HIS BROKEN HEART ANTIDOTE

THE MCKNIGHT FAMILY ROMANCES BOOK 5

LUCY MCCONNELL

ANNE-MARIE MEYER

ORCHARD VIEW PUBLISHING LLC

Copyright © 2020 by Lucy McConnell and Anne-Marie Meyer

All rights reserved.

No part of this book may be reproduced in any form or by any electronic or mechanical means, including information storage and retrieval systems, without written permission from the author, except for the use of brief quotations in a book review.

CHAPTER ONE
CARTER

There was nothing more satisfying than knowing that I'd helped someone. While taking off my mask and gloves, I could hear the nurses and anesthesiologist murmur to one another as the sliding door shut behind me. Surgery had gone well—exceptionally well.

Thank goodness.

I let out a breath and tossed my scrub covers, along with my mask and gloves, into the nearby garbage. Being exceptional might be difficult for others, but I was a McKnight, so it came with the slightly wavy hair and blue eyes. I'd felt the weight of my parents'—and the town of Evergreen Hollow's—expectations for most of my life. Compared to that, surgery was cake.

"Three points," I mumbled under my breath as I wandered to the sink and pressed my foot down on the bar. Water shot from the nozzles, and I dipped my hands in. After I scrubbed, I shook off the excess water and turned to grab some paper towels.

Grant's grinning face popped up in the window on the door. I smiled and shook my head. I knew the look in his eye. He had a plan for my Friday night that included him working the doctor angle for a few ladies and blowing off the stress. From my previous experiences with Grant and his plans, I knew I wasn't going to like it. Thrumming bass and strobing lights weren't my idea of a relaxing evening. I'd much rather kick back at my parents' cabin and drop a fishing line in the lake. That was where the real stress relief came from. No beeping monitors. No reputation to uphold. Just the bobber on the water and the sound of the birds in the trees.

Grant didn't move away from the door. I sighed and prepared myself for the long conversation ahead. He was my buddy, and I was his official wingman.

"Hey, man," I said as I headed into the hallway, walking fast like I had somewhere to go.

Grant was hot on my heels. "Appendectomy go well?" he asked, shoving his hands in the pockets of his scrubs.

I nodded. "Did you think otherwise?"

He chuckled. "You were named surgeon of the year."

My face heated from that reminder. I liked being the best at things, but I didn't need to be *known* as the best. Walking around with the last name McKnight already got me primo reservations and invitations to parties the mayor would love to get into; I didn't need another reason for my mom to draw attention to her doctor son. Being written up in *Doctors Today!* was more publicity than I liked.

My brother, Liam, on the other hand ... Bring out a camera, and he was all poses and flexing muscles. I supposed it came with the territory of being an NFL player, though I suspected that most of his antics were just him. He was always more carefree than I was—something I used to envy.

"I think your dad might have rigged the award," Grant said as he playfully punched me in the arm.

I winced, not from the blow to my arm, but the blow to my ego. Grant didn't know he poured salt into the paper wound of my deepest fear. Living in a small town was great, but sometimes I wondered what it would be like to work in a hospital my dad hadn't built—literally. His commercial construction company took on big projects, and he'd given the hospital a great deal on their last expansion, because he liked to give back to his community and the tax write-off was insane.

I kept quiet as we walked to the cafeteria. Grant moved quickly to lay out his plans for the night, acting as if I'd already agreed. Dressing up. Time at the club. Drive separately in case we met someone we wanted to spend more time with. Not that I was ever the one to take a woman home. I was a confirmed workaholic who put my career first. It came with the territory. I didn't have the luxury of dealing with dating drama. Grant handled it just fine by being emotionally unavailable to women. I couldn't do that, though. When I fell in love, it was going to be the build-a-life-together kind.

I thought about bowing out for the night, but I knew that it wouldn't make a difference what excuse I came up with; Grant wasn't going to allow me to say no, no matter how much I wanted to.

"I'm talking about babes upon babes." He grabbed one of the small, overly bleached trays and slipped it onto the metal counter in front of the protective glass shields.

Salads and premade sandwiches wrapped in plastic wrap sat behind the case. I wrinkled my nose at how sad and wilted the food looked. I was going to go with something hot today.

"Sounds like a party," I said as I grabbed my tray and turned away from Grant, eager to get a moment where I didn't have to chat about *babes upon babes*. "I'm going to grab something from the—"

A bar of some kind rammed into my back, making me jerk and stumble. It took a second for me to process what was happening. Then, searing hot pain shot through my body as I glanced behind me to see a red substance sliding all down my legs. "What the..."

I bit the inside of my cheek to keep the curse words from streaming forth. There was a kid with an IV drip not far away. I spun, slipping on red sauce.

My gaze cut to two dark green eyes glaring up at me through black-rimmed glasses.

I towered over the tiny woman, noting that her hair was pulled up into a bun at the top of her head. Which would have been strange if it wasn't so fetching.

"Why did you suddenly step out?" she demanded as she dropped to the ground and started scooping sauce back into the pot. She used her bare hands and was just as covered in the stuff as I was.

Thoughts finally formed back in my mind as I took a deep breath and crouched down. I started shoving the red sauce into a pile as I offered her a sympathetic smile.

That didn't thaw her icy demeanor. "This is a cafeteria. You should have looked behind you before you just jumped out of line." She scraped her tomato-colored hands on the edge of the pot before standing. Then she wiped the remaining sauce off onto her starch-white apron.

"Um …" I started, but then I pinched my lips together. She seemed to think that this was my fault, but that was not what had happened. I warred with myself, trying to decide if it was even worth attempting to fight her on this.

Her scowl deepened. "'Um' what?"

I wanted to meet her anger head-on, but she was just too dang cute, sitting there with her hands on her hips, looking like she was scolding a toddler, even though I was a good foot and a half taller than her and she was covered in red sauce. But she looked as if she were waiting for me to speak, so I decided if she was confident enough to dish it out, she should be able to take it. "You ran into me," I said as I leaned in to give her a playful smile.

Her eyes widened.

Betty, the regular cafeteria worker, appeared beside me with a mop bucket in hand. "I'm so sorry, Dr. McKnight. This was my fault. I asked Ellise to take the sauce out, and I should have done it myself." Betty's cheeks were pink as she smiled up at me, revealing the gap between her two front teeth. Some women paid lots of money to get that look, but Betty came by it naturally. I'd seen her granddaughter's smile.

I shook my head. "No harm, no foul," I said. "I'm used to dirty scrubs." I waved toward my now-splattered clothes.

Betty's cheeks reddened even more. But Ellise? Ellise didn't falter in her glare. I furrowed my brow as I studied her. She was really bothered by me, but I couldn't figure out why.

"A truce?" I asked as I extended my hand. When I realized that it was still covered in sauce, I brought it back and wiped it on my pants. I returned it to the space between Ellise and me, and she was no longer there. Instead, she was crouched down, dumping sauce by the handfuls into the garbage someone must have brought over.

"Dude," Grant said, as he nudged me with his elbow. "Ready?"

I glanced at my friend and then back to Ellise, who looked as if she was in no mood to speak. So I sighed, grabbed a peanut butter and jelly sandwich from the cooler behind me, and then sidestepped Ellise and Betty as we headed to the register.

Just before I was out of earshot, I heard Ellise mutter under her breath, "Typical."

I paused, wondering what she meant or if I should even respond, but then I brushed it off. Apparently, I'd upset her. I wasn't sure why I'd upset her to the level that she ignored me and fired insults, but I had regardless. And I was fairly certain that there was nothing I could do to change her predisposed notions about me. Still, it grated. I was the good guy. Maybe I should have been watching where I was going, but I'd done all I could to make up for ruining a pot of spaghetti sauce. It wasn't like her clothes stuck to the backs of her legs.

Grant found an empty table just outside of the cafeteria. I checked to make sure the red sauce wouldn't get on the chair before sitting down. Most of it was below the knee. We plopped down, and while Grant dug into his lunch as if he hadn't eaten in three days, I mindlessly picked at the crust of the sandwich I'd unwrapped. My gaze kept wandering back to Ellise and Betty.

They cleaned up in a matter of minutes, and soon, the floor was shining and any evidence that a huge sauce spill had occurred was gone.

I felt a tad disappointed watching Ellise disappear through the swinging door. She intrigued me. Not only because when she had no clue who I was—a rare find in a woman around these parts—but because, when Betty had called me *Doctor* McKnight, Ellise hadn't backed down.

It was ... refreshing, to say the least, and fascinating, to say the most.

"... and that's how I got a second family in Texas."

Grant's words drifted into my brain, and I snapped my attention over to him. "Your what?" I'd clearly missed something.

Grant scowled. "I was right. You're ignoring me."

Needing something to do, I shook my head as I took a big bite of my sandwich. "No, I wasn't," I said through a mouthful of bread and peanut butter.

He sighed. "Yes, you were. You missed my great punchline, all because you were staring at the new cafeteria chick."

I swallowed and then winced as my not-quite-chewed sandwich scraped my throat as it went down. "Was not," I wheezed.

He gave me a *yeah, right* look as he took a swig of his milk. "I don't blame you. She's cute."

I wrinkled my nose as I shook my head. "Don't say 'cute.' My mom uses that word when she describes the girls she's set me up with." I shuddered. "And they are cute, but only because they're barely older than Katie." Like the woman she'd set me up with not long ago. Bowling while she snapped pics for her social media posts was not my idea of a good time. I should have taken Katie; my six-year-old niece would have paid more attention to me and less attention to the number of followers on her latest account.

"Nice. Younger girls are nice." Grant bobbed his head.

I stared at my best friend. Since when had he started sounding like a pig? "No. Younger girls are wrong. I'm not ..." I shook my head. I was too old to date anyone in their twenties. "No," I finally said, hoping that would shut down the conversation.

Grant shrugged. "I'm telling you, don't set so many limitations for yourself. There's a vast ocean out there for a guy like you. You could have any girl."

I shoved the rest of my sandwich into my mouth and crumpled up the plastic wrap until it was in a tiny ball. "I don't want just any girl," I said as I went to stand. Grant followed. We walked over to the garbage, and I tossed my wrapper inside.

"Then what kind of girl do you want?" He took one last drink of his milk, returned the cap, and then tossed the whole bottle into the recycling.

That was a loaded question. It wasn't like asking someone what color of sweater they wanted or even what kind of car they liked to drive. A woman was mysterious and wonderful, confusing and scary. Honestly, I didn't know if I had a *type*. What did that mean, anyway? It wasn't like I could walk up to a vending machine and say, *I'd like a sporty woman today,* and just pick one out.

I turned, barely managing to catch myself from running into Ellise once more. Her rolling cart nearly shaved my stomach. She had a concentrated look on her face as she maneuvered the cart with one wobbly wheel, completely oblivious to my gaze. Once she rounded the corner of the hallway and disappeared, I turned my attention back to Grant.

"I dunno," I said as I shrugged. That movement caused the cold sauce to brush my leg. The desire to change rose up inside of me, so I made my way toward the locker room, where I could change. "Right now, no one." I pushed open the door and walked over to my locker.

Grant was behind me, with his eyebrows furrowed. He parted his lips as if to interject, but I held up my hand.

"But," I said in an exaggerated manner, "I'm sure I'll know her when I see her. If she even exists."

CHAPTER TWO
ELLISE

"Go change." Aaron, the hospital chef, sneered at my apron and scrub top, which were covered in red sauce, and pointed to the door.

Not "thank you for bringing me the food" or "I'd be lost without you." Nope. He wasn't grateful that I'd agreed to bring him the few plates he'd left behind when he'd hurried out of the kitchen ten minutes earlier. I'd reluctantly agreed to roll them to him despite the fact that Dr. McKnight had been staring at me as I'd walked by. I was a nice person, but Aaron seemed convinced otherwise. Either that, or he thought acting like the king of the kitchen gave him more authority. He was already the head chef; it wasn't like anyone was going to try and take that away from him, least of all me. I needed a job, and this one was available—end of story.

I bit back my *it wasn't my fault* defense, as he'd already moved on from the corner where I stood. So I sighed and did as he commanded. Two weeks into a new job in a new city wasn't the time to put up a fuss about his attitude. Besides, I wasn't at all sad to get out of the sticky top. The moisture was wet against my skin, and every time I passed under the air vent, I broke out in goose bumps—despite how warm I felt from the anger coursing through my veins from my run-in with Dr. McAwkward.

At least I'd learned one thing from my encounter with the clumsiest doctor on the planet—big egos were just as prevalent here as they were at Charlottesville General, my old home away from home.

I grabbed a scrub top from the lost and found and pushed my way into the locker room. The change from conversations to dead silence caused me to lift my head, and after a quick survey of the blue lockers and the urinals lining the far wall, a wave of dread washed over me, making it hard to swallow.

"Lost?" The most infuriating man on the planet—Dr. McSauce-Spiller—stood there in a clean pair of scrub bottoms and nothing else.

Nothing. Else.

I should have looked away. My entire face was bright red, but I couldn't help myself. Was I really human if I didn't take in the sculpted chest muscles and washboard abdominals in front of me? No.

But that didn't mean I needed to *take them in, take them in.* The female part of my brain didn't seem to get that memo. Instead, I stood there, gawking. Pure and simple. I made a complete fool of myself. The only thing worse would be if Betty rolled in with her mop and bucket to clean up my drool.

"I-I-I..." I what? I hadn't seen a body that beautiful since college? I wanted to run my hands over those muscles and lose my ever-loving mind? Loser Kyle, my ex-boyfriend who I'd left in Charlottesville, certainly didn't have abs like that. Instead, he had an insatiable need for women other than me.

His doctor friend chuckled. "I think you want the ladies' locker room?" He lifted a dark eyebrow that I'd highly suspected was shaped by a professional.

I shook myself out of my stupidity and stumbled backwards, grabbing for the door handle. Once I was safely on the other side of the door, I berated myself for being so weak. The man had caused a mess in the cafeteria, stepping into me and my spaghetti pan, and then blamed me. Only an idiot would allow her brain to be turned to mush at the sight of his tanned torso.

"Superwoman I am not," I muttered under my breath as I ducked into the next door over and changed out of my clothes. My face still burned with embarrassment when I exited the locker room five minutes later. I did a quick sweep of the hallway, and when I was sure Dr. McAbs was nowhere around, I hurried back to the kitchen. This was a big hospital; there was no reason for him to see me ever again. Even though I knew it was probably impossible to completely avoid him, a girl could hope. And right now, with my failed history at life, that was all I had. A small, miniscule glimmer of hope.

∽

I sniffed my hands as I walked the small concrete path from the parking lot to my apartment. They smelled like bleach. It was going to take a mountain of vanilla bean lotion to get that scent out.

The last thing I wanted to do after an eight-hour shift in the hospital cafeteria was go clubbing. But the minute I saw my best friend Brooke wearing a shiny pair of tight maternity pants and a red flowing top that didn't hide her seven-and-a-half-month pregnant belly, I knew where I'd be spending my evening.

I dropped my purse to the floor and slouched against the door. Some protest was in order, even if I knew I'd give in eventually.

"Come on," Brooke laughed as she waved her hand at my face. Apparently, I wasn't good at hiding my emotions. "Don't be like that. I'm doing this for your own good."

"My good would be a lavender bubble bath and Netflix." I headed for the fridge, determined to eat something that hadn't been on ice or under a heat lamp. Hospital food was good for sustaining life but not necessarily for taste. Although, after working in the cafeteria and seeing how much effort Aaron and the rest of the staff put into preparing and serving that food, my complaints took a nosedive.

Unlike a certain doctor who moved through the cafeteria like a Tasmanian devil. He couldn't even walk away and let me clean things up without getting himself more covered in the sauce and making me look even worse in front of Betty. My supervisor was kind, but she also bowed to the doctors as if they were demigods.

It wasn't like Dr. Dump-on-me was *that* cute. I chuckled at my new name for him. Each one was better than the last. Sure, he had blond wavy hair and the bluest eyes this side of Kentucky, but that didn't mean he could blame me for his two left feet.

I shook myself, grabbed a yogurt, and ripped off the lid.

"You can take a bath when we get back. Dancing will be fun, and you'll shed all that stress you're carrying around." She motioned toward my body as if I were nothing more than a pile of dirty rags.

I raised an eyebrow as I ate a spoonful of yogurt. "It's not that bad."

"It is." Brooke grinned. "I could hand you a shawl and a tabby cat, and people would think you're an 80-year-old with a knitting addiction."

I stood taller. "Fine. Just let me eat for a minute."

"Fine." Brooke leaned against the counter. "So who was it this time?"

"What do you mean?"

"I mean, the last time you came home under a rain cloud that dark, you'd stolen a doctor's parking spot and told him off."

I wrinkled my nose, thinking back to that day. "Same doctor, if you can believe it."

"Oh, I can believe it." She glanced up and mimicked me in a high-pitched voice. "And then he told me the space was his and I needed to move my car. As if! He doesn't own the hospital."

I laughed heartily. "I do not sound like that."

Brooke grinned and rubbed her belly.

"Are you sure you're up for dancing tonight?" My friend had a textbook beautiful pregnancy going, and I didn't want to mess it up by exhausting her. Too bad the romance leading up to the current situation had been a horror story. If only Greg could have been the type of guy Brooke deserved.

"I'm sure. Sitting at a computer all day is not good for my body. I need to move, and I miss dancing. Even if I'll look more like a parade balloon than a sexy ballerina, I'm good with that."

Before *Greg*, Brooke had been a dancer at our local theater back home. Hopefully, she'd get back to the stage one day, but her focus right now was getting this little one into the world healthy and happy.

I hated that she'd had to give up her dream, but I admired her for putting her baby first. We both had a new start in Evergreen Hollow—her working for a commercial construction company where they adored her and paid well, and me in the cafeteria where I was yelled at on a daily basis and my degree sat unused. Maybe one day I'd get back to labor and delivery, but it didn't feel like that was a possibility—not yet. "Then we'd better get you to the club. I'll change."

Brooke followed me into her room. "Weren't you wearing the ombré scrub top this morning?"

I groaned. "Yeah, Doctor Disaster spilled marinara sauce all over me, and I had to borrow this from the lost and found."

"Okay, ew." Brooke screwed up her face.

I threw the offensive mint-green top into the hamper and headed for the shower; I needed to rinse off the feeling of bleach tightening my skin. Brooke kicked back on the bed, scrolling through her phone.

Twenty minutes later, I popped out of the bathroom, with my hair out of the bun I'd put it in that morning and flowing in big, bouncy waves, and my mascara expertly applied. "I feel human again."

Brooke slid off the bed and grinned. "You're gorgeous. Let's go get you a date for next weekend so I can have a night off from being your wing woman." She bustled out of the room as fast as she could waddle-walk, trailing laughter behind her.

I shook her head. When it came to best friends, I'd won the lottery. My last relationship might have gone down in flames, but Brooke was hopeful I'd find someone again—someone so much better for me. I liked the sound of that. A man who built me up instead of tore me down sounded great.

The club wasn't far. Music spilled out the double doors, thumping an invitation for a good time. Neon lights above the door said *Blake's*.

I rolled my eyes. "Why do they name places like this after themselves?" I said, pointing up at the sign as the bouncer checked my ID.

The guy with steroid-pumped shoulders grinned down at me. "So you know who to ask for a good time, sweetheart." His gaze swept to Brooke as she thrust her license in his face. He jerked back in surprise at her baby bump. "Looks like you might already know that, though."

"Ugh!" Brooke shoved past him, muttering words that could describe farm animals.

We got inside, and I grabbed her elbow to get her to slow down. "Don't listen to him," I called over the noise. "He's an idiot."

Brooke nodded, but her shoulders were forward, as if she were trying to protect herself and the little one.

"Hey, you don't have to be ashamed for wanting this baby. She's yours, and you are going to make a great mother." I wished I could pour strength into Brooke. Yes, she'd picked the wrong man, but that didn't mean she had to give up on having a good life. Her new job would be perfect for balancing motherhood, and her boss was really understanding about maternity leave so soon after starting.

I was more than happy to try to build a life here, even if that meant facing my fears every day when I looked at my best friend. Any therapist with a reputable degree would diagnose me as crazy for the fact that I'd run from my job as a labor and delivery nurse right into a house where a patient existed—especially after the trauma I'd gone through. But I told myself that this was different. Brooke was different. And she was my friend, not my patient. The patient that I'd lost ...

Grief gripped my chest as I sucked in a deep breath. *Focus, Ellise,* I chanted, breathing out all the stress that had flooded my muscles and forcing them to relax.

Brooke took courage from my words. "Thanks." She lifted her chin and pushed her shoulders back. She seemed oblivious to my near breakdown, thank the heavens. "Let's hit the dance floor before my feet swell."

I waved her in the right direction. We found a space to call our own and started moving to the music. Several guys smiled my way, but I didn't try to encourage them. I wanted the night to last, and if I was cornered by an early mover, we'd have to leave to shake him off. I'd been there before and knew better than to jump in with both feet while the night was young.

The song changed, and I took a second to catch my breath. Brooke leaned close and spoke low. "See anyone you want to get to know better?"

I glanced casually over her shoulder, checking out the guys at the bar. As I scanned, a blond man spun on his stool. He leaned back on his elbows to survey the room, and our eyes locked. My stomach sank, my heart rate spiked, and I panicked as if the devil himself were sitting in that seat. "Crap!" I grabbed Brooke's hand and dodged behind a couple making out on the dance floor. "Hide me, now."

"Who …?" Brooke peeked around the couple.

I tugged her back. "Dr. Disaster is at the bar," I hissed. "Do not let him see me."

"Dr. Disaster is here?" She had an almost gleeful hint to her voice, and I inwardly groaned. My best friend had no loyalty whatsoever. Not when it came to attractive guys or torturing me.

"Don't look," I said as I huddled closer to her. "He'll come over here." Was it too late to sprint for the door? Would he notice?

I mentally slapped myself. Why would he notice? Guys like him didn't notice girls like me. I was just a stain on his incredibly immaculate scrubs.

"Um," Brooke giggled. "I think it's a bit late for that." She glanced over her shoulder at me and pointed in the direction where Dr. Disaster had been sitting.

I dropped my head back in defeat. Pulling myself together, I stepped around her to find the bluest eyes north of the equator laughing at me. "Dang," I drawled. Then I blinked and shook my head. What was wrong with me? I secretly pressed the pads of my finger to my inner wrist and felt my hammering pulse. I could be having a heart attack. Or a brain aneurysm. Those caused a spike in heart rate, right? That was the only explanation for my reaction to him. It couldn't be that Dr. McKnight looked delicious in his button-up shirt, jeans, and … were those cowboy boots?

My pulse beat faster. At this rate, my heart was going to give out. In this club. In front of Dr. Dynamite.

Heaven help me.

CHAPTER THREE
CARTER

"What did I tell you, man?" Grant said as he walked up behind me and shoved my shoulder. He'd just finished talking to a young brunette on the other side of the bar. He'd asked me if I wanted dibs, but I'd shrugged him off.

Picking up women at the bar wasn't really my thing. They wanted something more, or we'd spend the evening yelling at each other in an attempt to make a connection. I'd go home empty-handed and half buzzed only to get a screaming headache in the morning.

Which was why tonight, I was sticking to Sprite while Grant attempted to shove whiskey my way.

I turned to see Grant leaning his elbows on the bar. He was trying to flag down the bartender, who was busy flirting with a group of girls.

"Was it successful?" I asked, nodding in the direction he'd just come from.

Grant scoffed and shot me an *are you serious* look. "What do you think?"

I chuckled and shook my head, twisting my stool so I was now facing outward. "Success," I mumbled. Grant was batting a thousand right now. It seemed any girl he wanted instantly wanted him back.

As for me, my failures with the females didn't start with Ellise, but they ended right there. As did my thoughts each time they circled back to her. She'd blown me off, and now I couldn't get her out of my head.

Or my sight.

A woman who looked a whole lot like Ellise, with red curls that shifted as she talked, laughed with her friend. Her green eyes sparkled, even in the darkness of the room—like emeralds that were too good to be true. Her lips? They tipped up into a sexy smile as she perused the room. The moment our gazes met, they flattened to a line. She ducked down behind her friend and disappeared.

Determined to see if I was losing my mind or if in fact Ellise was here, I cleared my throat and stood. "I'll be right back," I said in Grant's general direction, not really caring if he heard or responded. He'd be fine on his own. I was just a place for him to land between collecting phone numbers anyway.

I weaved and sidestepped the couples who were half dancing, half using this time to make out, until I was standing in front of a very pregnant girl who grinned at me as if she knew something I didn't.

Before I could speak, Ellise appeared from behind her and sandwiched herself between us. "Hi," she said in a strained voice. Her cheeks were pink, which made the small dash of freckles across her nose stand out more.

"Hi," I responded. Then I flicked my gaze up to Ellise's friend, who was still smiling. "Carter," I said, extending my hand.

"Of course you are," the friend said. "Brooke. I'm Ellise's wing woman tonight."

"Brooke," Ellise hissed, and I turned my attention back to her.

"Wing woman?" I asked as Brooke dropped my hand. I couldn't help the smile that continued to spread across my lips. Ellise looked rattled, and I was kind of enjoying that. After her cold demeanor earlier today, I was grateful to see that she could show an emotion other than disdain.

"Ellise is single," Brooke piped up, stepping into my line of vision.

"All right, we're done here," Ellise said as she turned and started to push Brooke away from me. Brooke planted one foot and used her bulk to keep little Ellise from going anywhere.

"Can I buy you ladies a drink?" I asked, mostly to Brooke, who was still smiling. Ellise refused to look at me

"I'd love a drink." Brooke stepped to the side, effectively breaking Ellise's hold on her. She moved to stand next to me, and we both turned to look at Ellise.

"What do you say?" I asked, hoping she wouldn't opt out. Although Brooke was cute, I was interested in the fiery redhead in front of me. At least, I was interested enough to learn more. Brooke was doing her job as a wing woman, egging Ellise on with a jerk of her head.

Ellise looked as if she were going to decapitate the nearest person, but that only lasted for a moment before she let out a breath and glared in Brooke's direction. "One drink."

Brooke let out a "woo-hoo" as I led them over to the bar. I ordered three Sprites and then gathered the cups in my hands. Ellise and Brooke had moved to hover near a table where the occupants were gathering their things, and as soon as they left, the two of them plopped down at the booth, earning the glares of a few sweaty-looking women who seemed to have the same table in their sights.

When I got to the table with the drinks, Brooke cheered and grabbed a glass from me. Ellise sat there with her arms folded, sizing me up. She didn't move to take a sip of the Sprite.

"What's your plan?" she asked.

I was mid sip, and the directness of her question caused me to inhale sharply. In an effort not to spit the liquid all over her and the table, I swallowed quickly, ignoring the large bubble in my throat, and coughed. "What?" I managed.

"El," Brooke said as she leaned closer to her friend. "What are you doing?"

Ellise didn't break her gaze from me. Instead, she leaned over the table. "Why are you following me around? First the hospital and now here?" She leaned back. "What's your angle?"

"I'm so sorry. I think my friend may be having a seizure." Brooke offered me a sympathetic smile. "She doesn't talk to ... people much."

I allowed a smile to spread across my lips as I shrugged. "It's okay. Neither do I." I focused my smile on Ellise, hoping that eventually, I might wear her down.

She wasn't impressed with my status as a doctor, and the more I was around her, the more I realized that she didn't know who I was or what family I came from. It was refreshing and intriguing at the same time.

"I've worked at Evergreen General since I got out of residency, so I was there first." I gave her a small smirk and then waved toward the club. "I came with a friend."

"A friend?" Ellise asked, not at all attempting to hide the fact that she did not believe me.

As if that was all it took to summon Grant, he suddenly appeared and plopped down next to me. "This is where you ran off to," he said as he grabbed my Sprite and downed half of it. I stared at him as he returned the glass to the table. He furrowed his brow. "What?"

I widened my eyes and sighed.

Grant turned his attention to Ellise and Brooke. "Ah. Dr. Grant Pickering," he said as he reached his arm across the table. He shook Brooke's hand, and when he got to Ellise, he paused. "Cafeteria lady?" he asked.

Ellise's annoyance deepened as she turned to Brooke. "We should get you home. I mean, this can't be good for the baby." She moved to stand, but Brooke held on to her arm, which kept her rooted to the booth.

"I'm fine. It's rude to leave when someone bought you a drink." Brooke nodded toward the Sprite that Ellise hadn't even touched.

"Baby?" Grant asked, oblivious to the other parts of the conversation that had taken place since that statement.

"Yep," Brooke said, leaning back and motioning toward her swollen stomach. "Seven and a half months."

I peeked over at my friend, waiting for him to make some snide comment—or worse, a strange pickup line that he'd been wanting to try out. I didn't want to out the guy, but he had a notebook full of one-liners he used on a daily basis while I waited in line for lasagna or stroganoff. Of course, most of those were for Betty. He never left without her primping her gray hair at least once in the conversation. It was kind of cute, the way he took time to make the older woman blush.

"That's awesome. Good for you," he said, complete with a smile.

I blinked a few times as I tried to figure out what had happened to my friend. His response almost had me reaching for his forehead to check his temperature.

"Feel like getting some fresh air? It helped when my older sister was pregnant. This is stuffy." He waved his hand in front of his face.

Watching my normally piggish best friend turn into a gentleman was strange, and I must have done a horrible job hiding my shock, because Ellise grabbed on to Brooke to hold her back. "Why don't we just leave? Lots of fresh air back at our house."

Brooke grabbed on to Ellise's arm and slipped her entrapped one free. "I'll be fine. And you—" Her gaze snapped to me, and a smile teased her lips. "—need this." Her last two words escaped in a whisper, and she giggled as she turned and followed behind Grant, who was leading her outside.

Now completely alone with the woman who I was fairly certain hated me, I turned my attention back to Ellise and offered her a weak smile. "So …" I said as I wrapped my fingers around the glass and allowed the cool wetness to permeate my skin.

"Brooke," Ellise whispered under her breath as she returned her arms to her chest.

"Grant's a good guy. A little rough around the edges, but he'll take care of her," I said as I leaned in. "If that's what you're worried about."

Ellise's eyes widened as she stared at me. Her brows furrowed, and she took a deep breath. "What's your angle?" she asked again.

"Angle? Why do I need to have an angle?"

She sighed and dropped her hands to her lap. "They always do," she whispered. Then she pinched her lips together as she glanced up at me, and her cheeks hinted pink. She cleared her throat. "Listen, Carter. I'm sure you are a nice guy, and I appreciate your interest, but I'm not looking for a relationship."

I blinked a few times. Who said anything about a relationship? Ellise was distant and interesting, but I wasn't looking for a relationship either. Not after Holly. Not after I was pretty sure my heart didn't know how to fix itself long enough to attempt to love anyone else.

"Relationship?" I asked, the word sounding weird as it rolled off my tongue. "I'm not ..." I shifted in my seat and waved my hand between the two of us. "That's not what this is. I was just ..." How did I say *spending time with you because you seem oblivious to the fact that I'm a McKnight* without sounding creepy or complex? Realizing that there was no way to accomplish that, I took in a deep breath. "You seemed new to town, so I was trying to be hospitable."

Her eyebrows rose, and her lips parted into an O shape. "Hospitable?" she repeated.

I nodded and motioned toward my chest. "Self-appointed town welcome wagon."

She narrowed her eyes. "Welcome wagon?"

I flashed her a smile. "Yep."

She broke her gaze from me and glanced around the room, sighing as her shoulders slipped. "That's a relief," she said as her gaze found its way back to me. "Well, I think you can check this off your list. I feel sufficiently welcomed."

She shouldered her purse and moved to stand. Not wanting her to leave just yet, I moved to stand with her.

"Are you heading out?" I asked as I followed behind her. What was wrong with me? Why couldn't I just let her leave? We weren't friends. And according to her, we weren't even acquaintances. Why did I have this uncontrollable desire to follow after her, especially when she'd made it pretty clear that she had no desire to have anything to do with me?

Ellise paused and turned to look over her shoulder. Then she nodded and continued to sidestep the other club goers. "Yeah, it's time. If I don't get Brooke home soon, her feet will swell. Her blood pressure already worries me, and I want to do what I can to keep her healthy."

I listened to the way she spoke. It was clinical, as if she were a healthcare worker speaking to another one. I paused, allowing her words to mull around in my mind. Maybe it was from working at a hospital cafeteria. Did she absorb some of the jargon there?

"You care about your friend, don't you?" I asked as I stepped into the now-cool evening air. I took in a deep breath and reveled in the smell of fall that surrounded us. I loved Evergreen Hollow in autumn. The trees were changing colors, and the world seemed to slow down. The crispness of the air, mixed with memories of apple cider and hayrides, all came flooding back to me.

Ellise paused and then looked over at me. "Of course. She's my lifeline right now. I'd do anything to help her."

The hint of pain in her voice caused me to pause. It felt as familiar as my own heartbreak. Something had happened to her, something that had me suspecting that she had run away from whatever it was that had hurt her.

Her vulnerability under her cool exterior only piqued my interest more. I parted my lips to say something, but she extended her hand and her moment of weakness passed. She was back to being cold Ellise. "It was good to see you again. Thank you for the drinks and … awkward conversation." I met her gesture, and she gave our hands a few good shakes before she pulled back and wrapped her hand around her purse strap. "I think we can leave things here."

I furrowed my brow. "What?"

She eyed me and shrugged. "I feel sufficiently welcomed. There's no more need for us to this—" She waved toward the exterior of the building. "—again."

I parted my lips to protest, but she didn't wait for my response. Instead, she turned and headed in the direction of Brooke and Grant, who sat on a park bench not far away.

Before she was out of earshot, the desire to let her know that this wasn't the last time we were going to speak washed over me. So I did the stupidest thing I'd done in a while. "I'll see you around," I called after her retreating frame.

Ellise's back stiffened as she hesitated and then slowly turned to stare at me. Her eyebrows rose, and I could see the frustration in her gaze. She'd obviously wanted to break ties, but I wasn't having it. After all, I could be an asset to her. I knew the town and all of the people in it. I could help her find a place, people to hang out with and support her. She'd said she needed a lifeline, but maybe she just needed friends.

Not wanting her to think that I was in any way intimidated by her stare, I smiled and raised my hand to give her a short wave goodbye. She stared at my hand and then back to my face.

"I'll see you around," I said again, now that I had her attention.

Her lips tightened, and her hand grasped her purse strap as if she were holding on to it for dear life. Then she shook her head and said, "I doubt that."

I shrugged, but she didn't wait for me to answer. Instead, she hurried over to Brooke, and a moment later, they were walking side by side to the parking lot. I watched Ellise's retreat, and the image of her confused yet frustrated look entered my mind.

She was so determined to stand alone in the face of whatever storm she was riding out. I would be fine without her, but for some reason, I wanted to dig my heels in. I wanted to discover more about her. So despite the fact that she was convinced that we weren't going to see each other again, I knew better.

I wasn't done with Ellise. Not by a long shot.

CHAPTER FOUR
ELLISE

Dr. McKnight's persistence and his comment that he'd *see me later* hung with me over the weekend. I constantly looked over my shoulder, expecting him to pop up at any minute with his annoyingly perfect smile and can-do attitude.

Sheesh, the guy couldn't take a hint. Not in real life, and apparently, not in my head. He lingered, no matter how hard I brushed him off.

I'd been right—making eye contact with a guy at the club meant having to leave to shake him. Not that leaving was a bad thing. We got home at a decent hour, and Brooke was able to sleep a solid nine hours—all good things for her and the baby. She'd made a few comments about how nice Carter was, but after a sufficient glare from me, she raised her hands and laughed, saying that she got it. Talk of Carter was off the table.

However, morning meant something completely different. The gloves were off, and I winced when I found her in the kitchen.

"Morning!" Brooke chirped as she hit a button on the blender and filled the air with an unholy sound.

"What are you making?" I yelled.

"An energy smoothie." She turned it off, and my eardrums sighed with relief. "It's got all sorts of good stuff in it." She poured a glass and handed it to me before pouring herself one.

I sniffed and smelled bananas and apples. "What crunched?"

"Almonds and walnuts." She gulped hers down as I scanned the counter, trying to locate my purse and keys. Could I get out of here before we started the recount of the night before? "Do you think you'll see Dr. Dangerous today?"

Apparently not. I snorted. She'd started calling him that because she thought Dr. McKnight was a hottie. I agreed with her nickname only because he'd knocked me over—literally.

"Or maybe his friend?"

I froze. "His *friend*?" I slowly pivoted to take in her fake passiveness and lack of interest. "Grant?" I said his name with as much shock and dismay as I could pack into one word. "Brooke, no." I headed her way, waving my hands as if trying to stop a runaway truck. I guess, in a way, I was, because the look on her face was one I'd seen before. "He's a playboy. Everyone at the hospital knows it."

She lifted a shoulder. "He came across as sweet."

"That's what playboys do—they love-bomb you into thinking you're their one and only, and then they leave you high and dry. It's a game."

She studied me for a minute before she sighed and nodded. "Why do I always fall for the jerks?" There was a hint of emotion to her voice, and even though she wasn't saying it, I knew to whom she was referring.

I rubbed her back. She wasn't usually this emotional. I chalked it up to pregnancy hormones. "You haven't fallen for him. You had a conversation. Big difference."

She sniffed. "And texting."

My mouth fell open. "You gave him your number? You guys had, like, five minutes alone."

"Yeah, well, we've been texting and flirting. It's fun." She sniffed again and pulled her shoulders back. "I'll keep it casual. Don't worry."

"You know I will—it's what friends do."

She smiled. "I know. Now drink that smoothie and conquer your day."

I laughed. "I'm not sure what conquering the cafeteria looks like, but I'll give it a shot." I took another gulp of the smoothie. "It's really good."

She beamed. "Thanks."

I lifted my cup in cheers as I opened the door and headed out. The commute wasn't too bad, and I was soon in the cafeteria, dishing oatmeal next to Betty, who served French toast. She had a lot more takers than I did.

"How was your weekend? Did you do anything fun?" she asked during a lull.

"Brooke and I went to a club."

"I used to go clubbing, back when my hips had all the original parts."

I chuckled at her. "What was it like then? Did you have to park your dinosaur around the block?" She wasn't that old, but she was fun to talk to and tease with. I'd bet she'd been in high demand with the men back in the day, with her soft brown eyes and sparkling personality.

"Oh, you!" She whipped the rag off her shoulder and hit me with it. It had about as much impact as a butterfly. "I met Carl at a club, if you must know."

Carl was her deceased husband. She had a picture of him in his uniform in her locker. He was quite handsome. But then, it seemed like a man in uniform always was good-looking.

"Tell me about it?" I asked. I might be anti-love for myself, but that didn't mean I wasn't a sucker for a good romance.

Betty sighed. "Some other time. I'm out of toast, and it's time to take the mommies their breakfast." Mommies was her term for the patients in labor and delivery. She hoarded the job of serving them breakfast because she got to see all the beautiful new babies.

I let her have it without a fight. There was no way I wanted to step on that floor again. My family thought I should take another nursing job instead of settling for a spot in the cafeteria. After all, a nursing degree wasn't easy to come by. But I couldn't bring myself to apply.

I wouldn't even be at the hospital at all, except that this was the first place the temp agency had put me when I'd moved to town. The temporary position had turned to full-time after the first week. The hours were great, and the money wasn't horrible. It worked for me for now, and so I told my family to back off and let me get through things. They loved me, so they left me alone, but I still caught a note of disappointment when I talked to my mom.

Well, she wasn't the only one disappointed in how my life had turned out. But some things were handed to me and I wasn't sure what to do with them.

"I'd like some oatmeal, please," said a deep voice from the other side of the glass.

I glanced up from my deep thoughts and found myself staring into a pair of clear blue eyes. Crap! That was what I got for being distracted. "Dr. McKnight." I acknowledged his presence and dropped a gloppy, gooey ladle full of oatmeal into a plastic bowl and then passed it under the partition.

"You look nice." He took the bowl and placed it on his tray.

I resisted the urge to touch my hairnet. We didn't always have to wear them, but when we were serving food like this, it was a necessity. "Thank you for lying."

He laughed, his blue eyes sparkling.

I hated that I noticed that.

"It's not a lie."

I held up a gloved hand. "I'm not fishing for a greater compliment. I'm truly calling you out on your BS, which any girl in this getup is allowed to do."

He laughed easily. "Okay. Fine. What if I said the hairnet draws attention to your well-sculpted cheekbones?"

I flushed, coloring said cheekbones a dark red. The thing is, I've always loved my face. Not in a conceited way, but there are some people who are proud of their pert noses because they got the noses all the rest of us wanted, right? Well, I got the cheekbones others had to have implanted, and I loved them. "Thanks."

And then realization dawned on me. Was I flirting? I needed to leave. Now. His continued attention was too much. "Excuse me." I left my place and went into the kitchen, needing a breather.

"Perfect timing." Aaron didn't seem to notice my desperation as he handed me a tub full of tiny jellies and jams, butters and buttery spreads. "The condiment station needs to be filled."

I parted my lips to protest, but he didn't look in the mood. I doubted the excuse of *I'm running from the sexy and confusing doctor* was something he was interested in hearing. So I nodded, accepting the heavy tote.

"When you're done with that, come back for the ketchups and mustards."

"Will do." Conversations with Aaron just didn't happen. I'd quit trying to befriend him on the second day and just did what he said. We got along great after that. Although there were times when I wanted to tell him to watch his tone. I think he had a complex—like he thought he should be working in Paris or something and resented settling for a measly hospital. It was anything but a dump, with high-end appliances and plenty of work space. But there wasn't a lot of appreciation for what he did, and that could make anyone disgruntled.

I checked through the glass to make sure Dr. McKnight wasn't standing by the oatmeal anymore. I couldn't see him anywhere, so I pushed through the swinging door, using my backside as the battering ram to get it moving.

I headed for the condiments stand and began stacking the jams and jellies in their dispensers. I had to gather up a half dozen grape jams. No one liked the grape...

"Can I have one of those?" asked Dr. McKnight.

I moaned. "Sure." I only half turned, handing him three grape jams.

"Thanks." He stood there a moment, and I braced myself. "Have you always worked in a cafeteria?"

"Nope." I finished and scooped up my tote. I didn't get to hang around the kitchen long. Aaron thrust the second tote at me and pointed out the door. I almost stuck my tongue out at him. It wasn't like I could tattle on a doctor. No one would believe me if I said he was bothering me by asking for jam. That sounded dumb in my own head.

I pushed the door open, and Dr. McKnight waved at me from the condiment stand.

I marched over. "Don't you have patients to see?"

"I'm on break." He leaned his hip against the counter.

"You should go outside—it's pretty."

"I already ran my three miles this morning."

Of course he had. A man didn't get a body like his by eating Oreos. "Isn't your oatmeal getting cold?"

"I prefer it that way."

I huffed. "What do you want?"

He paused, considering his words. "To get to know you."

"Why? I've done nothing but try to blow you off. Am I some kind of a challenge to you?"

He shook his head, though the way his eyebrows drew down, I could tell he was considering my question. "You're ..."

His voice drifted off, and as much as I hated it, I paused, waiting for him to finish his sentence. Why did I care? I shouldn't care.

"Interesting," he finally said.

"Interesting?" What did that mean?

He pinched his lips together and nodded. "New and interesting."

I wasn't sure what he meant or if it was a compliment or insult. So I went a different route. "So you just want to get me out of your system or something?" I knew doctors. I'd been around quite a few. I'd learned that some doctors were self-centered. I hated accusing him of being that way, but really, it was for self-preservation. He needed to be a jerk if I was going to survive here at Evergreen General.

"It's not that, either." He ran his hand down his face. "I grew up here. I have a reputation—well, my family does. It's nice to meet someone who doesn't have my life history memorized."

I rolled my eyes. "Conceited much?" I tossed the last mustard package in the holder and headed for the kitchen again.

He dogged my heels. "That came out wrong."

Before I could go through the door, it swung open and Aaron handed me a tray. "Take this to room 534." He took my tote and replaced it with the tray.

My hands began to shake. *534. Fifth floor. Labor and delivery.* I steeled my nerves as I gathered my courage. I couldn't go up there. He couldn't ask me to do that. "But that's Betty's route," I whispered.

Aaron didn't seem the least bit interested. "This was called in late. Hurry," he barked, and then he shut the door behind him, leaving me standing there with shaking hands.

"Is he always that gruff?" Dr. McKnight asked. There was a hint of protectiveness in his voice, but I brushed it off. That was not what I should be focusing on right now.

I swallowed. "It's fine," I said, though I wasn't sure if I was answering his question or trying to talk myself into making this trip. I could do it. It was just dropping off a tray. I didn't have to do anything more than walk in and walk out. Robots did this kind of thing every day.

My vision focused on what was just in front of my feet. I wanted to protest when I heard Carter follow behind me, but I had no strength. It was taking all of my mental fortitude to just stand upright. The elevator dinged, and we stepped inside. Two nurses in pink scrubs got on after us. One of them pushed the button for the 5th floor.

"I'm wiped out," said the one closest to me.

"Twelve-hour delivery—that's tough."

I started to shake, and my mind went back to another delivery room, not long ago. I was watching in horror as the doctor made the wrong call. The warm smell of blood and the musty smell of amniotic fluid filled my senses.

The nurse continued, "I thought the poor mom was going to pass out at the end. But she was determined not to have a C-section, and the baby was fine—right up until the last minute."

"What happened?"

"His heart rate dropped—scary fast. Dr. Rasband did an episiotomy. She delivered like that." She snapped her fingers.

The sound mixed with the silverware clanking on the tray. Two strong hands wrapped around mine, and I blinked, trying to focus on the face in front of me.

Carter pulled the tray out of my hands and handed it to one of the nurses. "Can you take this to room 534?"

"Sure." She winked at him just as the elevator doors opened on the fifth floor. They stepped off, leaving me alone with Carter.

Relieved of my burden, I sank against the back wall. The doors shut, and Carter pressed a button. I wasn't sure which button, but right then, I really didn't care which floor he was taking me to. I closed my eyes, trying to bring myself back to the here and now and to lock those horrible memories back in the box that they belonged in.

"Hey now." His voice was calm and his hands strong as he ushered me out of the elevator and onto the … roof? Why were we on the roof? The sunlight blinded my eyes for a moment, and I cringed.

Then the shaking began in earnest. And to my humiliation, tears began to fall. "I'm cold," I bit out as I quivered.

Carter paused, dipping down to meet my gaze. I could see hesitation in it, as if he wanted to do something but was unsure of how I would take it. With the way I was feeling, he could wrap me in bubble wrap and ship me to Guam and I wouldn't fight him. I was emotionally and physically spent.

But what he did next shocked me. Suddenly, he wrapped me up and held me close, rubbing his hands over my back and arms to create heat. I stood there, stunned. What was I supposed to do? Did he do this with everyone he brought up here? Was I supposed to hate this? Was it bad if I liked it?

He'd become the strength that I hadn't known I needed. I pushed out all thoughts and decided to just act. I was tired of overanalyzing everything. Right now, I just wanted to stop thinking. So I leaned into his solid form. After all, I was banking on the fact that he'd see me fall apart, and I was fairly certain he'd run for the hills. I didn't blame him.

Some days I wished I could run away from myself. "Sorry," I hiccupped.

He pulled me tighter. "Nothing to be sorry about."

"I didn't mean to fall apart." I stepped back, feeling more myself with the autumn sun on my skin and the bright light of day reminding me that I was here, now, and not then and there. "I'm better, thank you."

He let me go. "Who's lying now?" he gently teased.

I swiped under my eyes. "Really. I'm good. Thank you for your help." I hoped that he'd take the hint and let me be alone for a few minutes. No such luck. Then again, this guy didn't get hints. I was going to have to be more forward with him. "I need a minute. If you could just …" I waved toward the door.

He shook his head. "I can't leave you up here alone."

"Why not?" I demanded. Did he think I was going to do something stupid like jump off the roof?

"Because you can't get back in without a key." He lifted his lanyard, which had his ID that also worked as a key on the electronic door locks.

"Oh." I slumped.

"We all get overwhelmed with the job—medical care is tough physically and mentally." His words lingered in the air, and I could feel the intensity of his stare as he studied me.

I needed to lighten the mood. "Uh-huh. Why do I feel like you're leading up to something I'm not going to like?"

He grinned, making his eyes crinkle in the corner. "Because I am."

I laughed. "Well, at least you're honest about that. Lay it on me."

"We all have to find a way to detox from the stress—if not, it takes a toll."

"So? Should I start running?"

"Yes, and I have just the place."

"Oh? Is this part of the welcome wagon? Show me all the good running trails?"

"Something like that. So how about it? Wanna see the best place in Evergreen Hollow to de-stress?"

I hesitated. But then I thought of the way I'd felt in the elevator, the fears that overcame me—and I wanted to be free from them. The counselor at my old hospital said that keeping my stress levels down was key to preventing a PTSD episode. "Okay, doc. When and where?"

He smiled so big, you would have thought he'd won the Boston Marathon. "I'll work out all the details. We can meet here and ride out together." He ushered me toward the door and swiped his name tag. The cool, sterile feeling air hit me in the face, and I cringed. I used to love walking into the hospital. Back when I loved my job. Maybe I could get back to that someday. But not if I didn't figure out my head first.

We arranged a time to meet that worked for both our schedules as we rode the elevator back down. I moved to step out, but he grabbed my arm, halting my retreat. "Ellise?"

"Yes?" I glanced down to where his hand wrapped around my arm. A warm, pleasant tingling happened there. Weird.

"Call me Carter." He winked and let go, the door shutting on my no doubt surprised face.

"Carter," I said out loud. For some ridiculous reason, a smile grew across my lips. I pinched them together as hard as I could. I wasn't this kind of girl. I wasn't swayed by sexy guys who smelled like a mix of musk and spice. I was stubborn and reserved. Yet I couldn't help my thoughts as they returned to him.

He'd offered me something no one at my old hospital had offered —support. Maybe it was just one outing, but at least he hadn't left me alone to deal with my memories.

That was a good enough reason to trust him. And I was bound and determined to ignore any lingering thoughts that emerged after he'd held me close. Because right now, those kinds of thoughts would get me into trouble, and I'd had enough of trouble.

CHAPTER FIVE
CARTER

Five o'clock rolled around, and I was anxious to get out of the hospital and on with the evening I had planned. I said goodbye to a few nurses who smiled and nodded at me as well as a few doctors. Dr. Hannover looked like he wanted to talk more, but I wasn't interested in hearing about his latest golf game or the driver he'd bought from whatever pro toured through town. I needed to change, get in my car, and head to my parents' house.

My pulse thrummed with anticipation of spending more time with Ellise. I didn't want to think too much about why I was so drawn to her, but because my brain worked like that, it was all I could think about.

Anything was better than thinking about Holly.

Ellise and Holly were complete opposites. Holly was like a spider monkey, clinging to me at every turn. I couldn't get Ellise to hang around. Every minute with her was like a trophy.

Holly had worked hard to control me and my time. She had visions of what I should be doing with my life, with my evenings, with her. And she wasn't afraid to put her foot down, either, in a full-on pouting session or by plucking my guilt strings. One of her favorite tunes to play was that I had a responsibility to my family to uphold their reputation. It wasn't until I was so strung out by her demands that I realized she was the one trying to live up to the McKnight standards and failing. My family might be successful, but we were all about caring for one another. Holly was all about herself.

I could see that now, but at the time, I'd been devastated to lose her. Breaking up had felt like tearing off a limb. The crazy thing was, I'd grown into a whole, more complete version of myself. I felt like I was able to see others better.

Now, I was seeing Ellise.

I'd never had to work so hard to get time with a woman, and though the challenge was intriguing, there was more to my excitement than conquering a mountain. She'd seemed so vulnerable, so broken earlier and I wasn't going to lie, this was an onion I wanted to peel.

I'd seen similar reactions to situations from my brother Mason, who was currently getting help for PTSD from his military service. Healthcare workers were not immune to traumas that hung with them and caused flashbacks, nightmares, and panic attacks. I knew of quite a few doctors who'd lost their edge because of it. So the fact that Ellise was facing this—and, from what I could tell, facing it alone—caused a desire to help to rise up inside of me. My brother had someone to lean on: his amazing girlfriend, Sadie. Sure, Ellise had Brooke, but it looked like Ellise spent more time taking care of her friend than taking care of herself. She needed a champion, a shoulder to lean on. I could be that for her.

Plus, she was sassy and seemed as if nothing I did fazed her. She wasn't impressed with my family status or my looks. And I liked it. It was refreshing to finally be the one to pursue the other. It made me feel like a man.

A nervous feeling grew inside of my gut as I pulled into my parents' driveway—one step closer to Ellise. Only this was a big step. Getting in and out of my parents' house with the key to the cabin and without the third degree would take a miracle.

The sun had set behind the house, illuminating both stories and the intimidating roofline and casting the driveway in shadow. As much as I loved my parents, living in their shadow was cold and suffocating. It was as if I was constantly under a microscope—no matter what I did, it was always seen through the McKnight family lens. Holly had known that and exploited it. I wished getting rid of her got rid of all those feelings, but some things lingered.

My siblings dealt with it in their own ways. Mason had joined the Army. Penny had spent her teen years rebelling against everything our parents stood for. Liam took the reputation and ran with it—all the way to the NFL. He played up the rich-kid heartbreaker role with pizzazz. One might think he was well adjusted, but he had a new girlfriend every two months and didn't let people close. Lottie ... well, she had a double dose of issues, being the youngest of us all. Until recently, she'd pushed herself to catch up to her older siblings. I liked the calming effect that her fiancé, Jaxon, had on her.

I sighed as I pulled open the driver's door and stepped out. Even though people thought we had the perfect family, I couldn't help but think we were a bag of mixed nuts. I was allowed to think that, though, because I'd had to grow up sharing a bathroom with these people.

The soft autumn breeze washed over me, and I inhaled all things that reminded me of childhood and a simpler time.

I pushed open the front door and walked in, only to be hit with children's laughter and shouting coming from the living room. I chuckled at the familiar yell from my niece Katie that meant she was in a dance battle to the death.

After kicking off my shoes, I padded into the room to find Katie and Parker, Mason's soon-to-be stepson, in front of the TV. They battled each other on some video game, and both were jumping and shouting in excitement.

I chuckled as I tousled the hair on their heads. They complained and swatted my hands away in annoyance.

"Carter." Penny's voice drew my attention to the other side of the room, where she was standing in the doorframe with a metal bowl in her arms and an apron on. She had the best mom face as she glowered at me for disrupting the game. She must have put them in here to get them out of her hair for a minute.

I raised my hands and made my way over to where she stood. She and Chris were back after their intimate wedding and his latest commercial shoot, and they were spending time with Mom and Dad before they left for the start of his movie being filmed in Florence. Penny also checked in on Chris's grandma. They'd hired a new nurse to be with her full-time, but for Penny, taking care of her needs was a labor of love.

It was good to see my sister. We used to work at the hospital together and met up for lunch a couple times a week. Since she'd gotten married, I'd missed her. I pulled her into a hug despite her protests and efforts to shift the bowl she carried to her other hip.

"Looking good," I said as I planted a kiss on her head. She snorted and shook her head as she stepped back

"I haven't showered. Those chitlens demand too much of me." Her hair was pulled up into a bun, but wisps fell down around her face, and she emphasized her exhaustion with a dab of her wrist to her forehead.

"That bad, huh?" I asked. Despite being a beautiful woman, she looked tired. Bags under her eyes and a general sense of being worn out awakened the doctor inside of me. I set her bowl down on the counter and my fingers found her pulse. I studied her, noting her flushed cheeks against her pale skin and the few pounds she'd lost.

Something was wrong.

"Carter, I'm fine," she said, her voice barely a whisper.

I shook my head and helped guide her to the barstool. I pressed down on her shoulder, and she obliged me and sat. After taking her pulse and temperature with the back of my hand, I moved to listen to her breathing with my ear pressed to her back. I had a bag of emergency supplies in my car. I should have gotten one for Mom's kitchen too. That was a mistake I planned to rectify—and soon.

"Carter," she protested. I could hear the rumblings of her voice through her chest.

"Shhh," I whispered as I adjusted to listen to another spot.

She turned suddenly and bopped me on the head. "I'm pregnant," she whispered.

I paused, my entire body freezing in place as I tried to process what she'd said. Then I straightened and asked, "You're what?"

A smile spread across her lips, and I could see that even though she was tired, she was happy. "I'm pregnant," she said softly.

"Pregnant?"

I must have been too loud, because she stood and pressed her hand against my mouth. Glancing around the room to make sure we were still alone, she hissed, "You're the only one who knows. We haven't told the family or Katie yet."

I chuckled, feeling honored that I was the first to find out about the new addition to the family. "And you trusted your brother with this information. I don't know what to say." I pretended to wipe a tear away.

Penny swatted my shoulder. "You made me tell you. If I didn't stop you, you'd have called an ambulance."

I nodded. She was right. I probably would have. I took my family's health seriously.

"Carter, you're here," Mom said as she rounded the corner. She had on her reading glasses and a book in her hand.

"Mum's the word," Penny whispered as she moved to gather her bowl back up.

I smiled, unable to stop myself, and turned to give my mother my full attention. "Yeah, I just stopped by to see if I can get the keys for the cabin." I moved forward to give her a quick kiss on the cheek.

"The cabin?" Mom asked. "Don't you have to work tomorrow?"

I shook my head and followed her over to the cupboard where all of the keys hung—neatly labeled and organized. "Nope. I'm off. I'm looking for some R&R." I decided I should probably leave out *who* I was spending my R&R time with, considering my mother's hopes that I'd settle down and find a bride sooner rather than later. I wasn't opposed to doing so—I just hadn't met the right one. And the women Mom thought were good matches ... well, let's just say that many of them were in love with having the last name McKnight.

Mom removed the cabin key and turned to hand it to me. "Are you available this weekend?"

I wanted to stop the groan that boiled up inside of me, but I couldn't. It came out low and throaty.

Mom's eyebrows went up as she studied me. "You don't know what I was going to say."

I shot her a look. "Yes, I do. You want to set me up with one of your country club friend's daughters." I took the key from her before she could reply. "I'm not interested."

"Carter," Mom said as I hurriedly kissed her cheek and turned to leave.

"Mom, leave him alone," Penny called out.

I didn't turn around but waved at her from over my head. "Thanks, Pen," I said as I made my way through the living room, called out a goodbye to my niece and nephew, and then hurried out to my car before Mom could catch up with me.

Once I was on the road, I let my shoulders relax and the stress of dodging another horrible setup leave my muscles.

I paused at the stoplight just as my phone chimed. Ellise's name came up on the dash display. She'd been reluctant to give me her phone number when I'd seen her at lunch—I could see her reservations starting to grow—but I hadn't let that dissuade me. Instead, I'd insisted and she'd finally relented.

But now, seeing her number flash across my screen had me panicking. Was she going to cancel?

Not wanting her to blow me off through a text, I pressed the call button on the steering wheel. It rang a few times before she picked up.

"Um, hello?"

I could hear the hesitation in her voice. It was a good idea to call. She couldn't reject me to my face—er, voice to voice—right?

"What's up? I saw you texted, but I'm driving and couldn't look." I decided to play it casual, as if we called one another several times a day. The light shifted to green, so I pressed on the gas just in case she could hear the car.

"Oh." She was quiet for a second.

"You're not canceling on me," I said, teasing.

She chuckled, but it sounded more forced than anything else. "Thing is—"

"She's coming." Brooke's voice came through the phone as if she were standing next to Ellise.

"I've got this handled," Ellise said, her voice muffled as if she were trying hide the phone in her shirt and keep it away from her friend.

"No, you don't!" Brooke whisper-yelled.

I laughed. I really liked Brooke. She was straightforward and sweet. And I was glad that Ellise had someone in her life like that.

Ellise must have heard my laugh, because she cleared her throat and said, "Anyway, I'm calling because I just don't think I can meet up with you at the mysterious place tonight."

"What? This isn't what we talked about." Brooke must have leaned in closer to the phone, because her voice was infinitely louder. "Don't listen to her, Doctor Dangerous. She's freaking out but wants to come."

"Excuse me." There was a scuffle on the phone, and I could only imagine that Ellise was attempting to get away from Brooke.

Dr. Dangerous? Was that what they thought? That I was some serial killer who lured women into the woods?

"Don't let her talk you out of this." Brooke's voice was quiet, and a moment later, I heard a click that made me wonder if Ellise had retreated to a room.

"I'm sorry about that," Ellise said, her voice breathy.

I shook my head as I pulled to the side of the road. I wanted to give all my attention to this conversation. "It's fine. I like Brooke."

Ellise's laugh was soft, and I could hear the affection she had for her friend in the tone. It made me smile. I liked Ellise. I could picture myself teasing with her about which movie to watch, running around the house playing keep-away with the remote. That was the kind of spice missing from my life.

"So, about tonight."

"I'll see you there," I said.

Ellise was quiet, and I could tell that she was trying to come up with a reason to get out of it.

"Hey, I get it. You don't want to spend the evening with a stranger, but I can guarantee you that my intentions are only honorable, and I have nothing on my mind besides helping a fellow healthcare worker out." The words tumbled from my lips before I could police them. And when she didn't respond right away, I began to fear that I might have said too much.

It wasn't until she sighed that relief finally flooded my body. She seemed as if she were relinquishing whatever fears she'd built up and might actually agree to meet me. I knew that we were strangers and she had no reason to trust me, but I couldn't deny the fact that I was drawn to her.

"I don't know," she whispered. Just before I parted my lips to try to convince her, she said, "But I guess I can come for the evening. It's only a few hours, right?"

I nodded. "Yep. Just a few hours."

"Hmm." Then she sighed again. "Text me the address, and I'll meet you there. I'd prefer to drive in case I need to leave."

I scoffed.

"To be here for Brooke," she hurried to respond.

I smiled and nodded. "I get it. I'll text you the address and see you there."

"Yep."

Once we hung up, I hurried to text her the address and then got back on the road. I'd pulled off for a Coke and some gas at the only station before civilization ended and the mountains began. I'd always liked stopping there as a kid and getting a candy bar to eat on the dock.

Spending time up here on my own as a teenager had helped alleviate the pressure to get perfect grades. I'd announced early on that I wanted to be a doctor, and my parents had pushed me to do all I needed to do to follow that dream. I knew they were doing what they thought was best for me—and obviously it worked out, because I'd gotten my degree. But there were times I'd wanted to be seen as just their kid and not the future doctor of the family—that was when I escaped to the cabin.

I grabbed a dozen candy bars, not knowing which one Ellise liked, and carried the bag out to the car.

It was only a half-hour drive to the front door, and when I got there, I opened the place up. The air was stuffy, and there was dust on the kitchen counter. Mason had been here last, so I knew it had been wiped down before he left—you could take the man out of the army, but you couldn't take the army out of the man.

I opened the windows to let in some fresh air and started a pot of coffee. I wanted Ellise to feel the calm here. A lot of that came from breathing fresh air, hearing the leaves rustle and the birds talk to one another. A few minutes into the coffee gurgling, the house smelled of hazelnut and late-evening air.

I checked the clock. She should be here any minute. The turnoff wasn't hard to find, so she shouldn't get lost.

There was a bite to the temperature, so I pulled a sweatshirt from the closet and slipped it on. I paced the braided rug by the front window and eyed the coffee. I didn't want to drink it all before she got here, and in my agitated state, I might down the whole pot. I tried not to, but I had so much pent-up energy that there was no way I was going to be able to sit still.

Fifteen minutes passed by, and what was left of my coffee was cold. I sighed as I rinsed out the mug and set it down next to the sink. I pushed my hands through my hair as I stared at the floor.

Was I an idiot for hoping so hard?

I blew out my breath and tipped my head up and closed my eyes. The truth was, yes, I was an idiot. A huge, colossal idiot. I'd hoped that I could finally be friends with Ellise, put myself out there again after Holly had torn me up. But maybe I was hoping for too much.

I started moving around the house, putting things back the way I'd found them. I went to close the front window when a pair of headlights stopped me in my tracks. Then, a moment later, they slid into the driveway and turned off.

She was here.

I cleared my throat and began to move around the cabin undoing everything I'd just done. I hoped I looked calm, but if she could see me, I was a complete spaz.

By the time there was a knock on the front door, I was sweating and beet red. I growled as I took in a few deep breaths.

Get a grip, I chanted in my head.

After a few tight fists to help relieve my anxiety, I moved to open the door. Ellise stood on the stoop, her eyes wide and looking completely beautiful. Her hair was down, and she wore a green turtleneck that accentuated her red hair and pale skin. She had on jeans and knee-high boots.

"Welcome." I tried not to stare as I stepped back to let her into the cabin, but my effort was in vain. She was breathtaking. And here. This was a good sign. "Let me take that," I said as she shrugged out of her jacket. She nodded, and in my effort to help her, my hands brushed against her shoulders. Even though her skin was covered, jolts of electricity shot through my body at her warmth.

My heart picked up speed, and I tried all I could to shush it. There was no way I was going to allow those thoughts to emerge. She was here as a *friend*, and that was it. She was trusting me to be a gentleman, and I was going to be one and prove that I wasn't Dr. Dangerous. "Why don't you go on out to the deck, and I'll pour a coffee?"

"Thanks." She disappeared through the French doors, and I jumped into action.

Once her coat was hung and a cup of coffee poured, I grabbed my mug and the bag of candy bars and followed her out onto the deck.

"That's a whole lot of chocolate." She motioned to the bag sitting on the rail.

I lifted a shoulder. "A man's got to have a selection."

She smiled softly.

"Actually, I didn't know what you like, so I bought a bunch. Anything speaking to you?"

She reached for the chocolate bar filled with caramel. "This one."

"Good choice." I grabbed the peanut butter cups.

We sipped and stood there in silence, surveying the forest around us. It didn't take long for nature to work its magic. The tension in her shoulders eased, and she leaned on the rail, allowing it to take her weight.

"It's beautiful here," she whispered as she brought her mug up to her lips and took a sip.

"Yep," I said, dropping my gaze so she wouldn't sense my double meaning. I was aware of a lot of things in that moment: the dropping temperature, the owl hooting to the east, the gentle lapping of the lake as fish jumped for their dinner. But what I was mostly aware of was her.

When I glanced back at her, I saw her studying me with interest, but as soon as our gazes met, she dropped hers back to the scenery.

Intrigued by what she was thinking, I chuckled. "What?"

She pinched her lips together and shook her head. "Nothing."

I turned, leaning one elbow against the railing of the deck and focusing my attention on her. "Tell me."

She shook her head. "It's nothing."

I raised my eyebrows. "There's an *it's*?"

She furrowed her eyebrows for a moment as if she were chewing on what I'd said, but then she laughed. "You pick up on everything, don't you?"

"Hey, *Medical Times* didn't name me doctor of the year for nothing." It was a line—and a horrible one at that. But at least it got a smile from her. That was a victory in my book.

"What? *Medical Times*?" She shook her head. "You made that up."

I shrugged. "Or did I?" It felt nice, talking to Ellise. Any previous date would have giggled, swatted my arm, and leaned in close. But not Ellise. And it was her indifference that drew me to her. Not wanting our relationship to be just jokes and vague comments, I moved to lean into her. "In all seriousness, you can say anything. It's part of the magic of this place. No worries."

Her eyes were wide, and for the first time since I'd met her, I sensed vulnerability there. She was nervous about something. And that thought had my heart pounding.

And then, slowly, cautiously, she lowered her guard. "Thank you," she whispered.

Confused, I furrowed my brow. "For what?"

"Earlier. In the elevator. Thank you for saving me."

I felt as if I could fall into the depths I saw in her eyes. She'd been hurt in the past; I could see that. And in the elevator, when I'd been sure she was going to faint from how pale her skin was, I'd finally understood that something had been going on. Something had happened to her.

I shrugged as I moved to rest both elbows on the railing and took in a deep breath. "Of course. I'm not as bad of a guy as you think."

She scoffed, and I squinted in her direction. Her smile dropped. "I don't think you're a bad guy."

"Really?"

She pinched her lips together and nodded.

Wondering how far I could push her, and wanting to see if she'd loosen up, I tipped my body closer to her. "So, what kind of guy do you think I am?"

She studied me. And just as I was pretty sure I was going to die from the silence, she parted her lips to speak.

A shrill ring filled the air, and we both jumped apart. My heart pounded, and I swore I saw Ellise's cheeks flush. But before I could confirm it, she glanced down at her phone and her skin paled. "I have to take this."

I motioned for her to do so, and she ducked back inside the cabin, her phone pressed to her ear.

I turned back to the scenery to give her some privacy, my thoughts racing faster than I cared to admit. What had she been going to say?

CHAPTER SIX
ELLISE

"I don't know. My stomach feels hard, and then it doesn't."

I held the phone closer to my ear. The sound of blood rushing through my veins threatened to block out everything else. This was Brooke. I needed to pull it together for her. "Are you in pain?"

"No—just uncomfortable."

She probably had contractions, but I wouldn't know until I was there, timing them. "Shoot. Okay, I'm on my way."

"I'm scared."

"I know, honey. It's going to be okay. Please lay down until I get there."

"I'm on the couch."

"That's good."

"I'm hungry." Her voice was small and pouty, like a kid who'd been sent into time-out.

I laughed. She was always hungry, so that was no way to judge if she'd gone into early labor or not. "Just hold off on snacking. I'm not that far away." Just a half hour and one awkward goodbye. We hung up, and I headed back out to the deck where Carter waited. "Hey."

He choked on the peanut butter cup he'd just popped in his mouth.

I smiled. It was funny that I'd caught him off guard after his smooth moves earlier. Maybe he didn't have it as together as he believed he did—which made him all that much more attractive.

I never liked the guys who always knew what to say and who could walk through a wind tunnel and come out with perfect hair. They were too perfect, and I kept my guard up, knowing that their act would slip at some point. It always did, because perfection was a lie. With guys like that, it was worth buying popcorn and blocking out an evening to watch it all fall apart, because they did it big. Like divas.

"Listen, I'm sorry to cut this short, but I need to go." I was kind of sorry. I'd just started to relax, listening to the wind rustle high in the trees. Not to mention I hadn't had a chance to enjoy my chocolate bar.

Carter's expression fell slightly. He recovered his smile quickly and cleared his throat. "Really?"

I chewed my bottom lip, contemplating his sincerity as I glanced around the deck. This wasn't the kind of place where a single guy brought a woman he was trying to romance. I mean, he could, but it was too homey to put off that I'm-trying-to-seduce-you vibe. The blanket thrown over the back of the couch was tied with care, and the number of chairs on the deck indicated it was used by a lot of people. This was a special place to Carter, and I was surprised he'd been willing to share it with me.

Which all brought me around to the idea that he really did want me to stay. As much as I didn't want to like it, I did. It was nice to have someone who cared about where I was. And it made me miss being in a relationship ... almost. I wasn't ready to hand over my broken heart to this doctor or anyone else.

Thank goodness I had a great excuse to get out of there. If I stuck around, I might do something I'd regret later. "Yeah. Brooke needs me back home."

Carter nodded fervently as he dusted off his hands. Then he glanced around quickly and snatched the bag of chocolate off the rail. "Here, take this."

I eyed it warily. That was a lot of chocolate.

He tucked his hand in his pocket. "You didn't get the full

experience up here. Those are best eaten at the end of the dock watching the sunset, but chocolate's always good for the soul."

"Is that your medical opinion?" I reached for the bag, my fingers brushing his of their own accord. A tingle shot up my hand, and I bit my lip in an effort to ground myself. There was no way I wanted to drop the bag and for Carter to read into more than the fact that I was nervous about Brooke—not about him, and certainly not about the way he made my stomach somersault.

He chuckled. "Definitely. I'd prescribe chocolate and sunsets for you any day."

My chest warmed. "I like that. Thanks." I headed inside, and he followed me, retrieving my jacket from the hall and helping me put it on like a true gentleman. I wasn't sure what I should make of his actions. One minute, I thought things were on an even keel and we could be friends. But then my heart had to go and race when our skin touched, and I wondered if I was the only one feeling it.

I wished I could be cured by a trip to a cabin, and that I'd be able to explore all these feelings and tingles. But my damage ran deeper than the lake.

As I drove away, my eyes darted to the rearview mirror over and over again. Carter stood there in the drive, his hands tucked into his pockets and his head down as if he'd failed somehow.

I didn't like that one bit, but I couldn't pinpoint why it bothered me so much. He was just a guy I'd met at work. Nothing more.

So why did my heart go out to him?

I made it home in record time and found Brooke on the couch, right where she said she'd be. There was a timer beeping in the kitchen.

"Can you turn that off? It's driving me insane," she half-barked.

I ran in there and hit the button on the microwave, thankful for a few more seconds where I didn't have to tap into the part of my brain that handled mommies and babies. "Did you get up?" I called as I opened the door and looked inside. There was a Lean Cuisine, overbaked and gelled. I tossed it in the trash.

I set the bag Carter had sent home with me on the counter. I didn't even realize I'd grabbed it off the front seat of the car. Maybe I'd wanted the small reminder of him—subconsciously, of course. My conscious didn't need Carter. Nope.

"No. I started it before I called you. I didn't dare get up to get it, because every time I move, my stomach goes as hard as a bowling ball."

My stomach dropped. It was time to go into nurse mode and help my friend. I just … I just wanted to get it right. Even though I'd known the doctor had been doing the wrong thing for that patient, I hadn't stood up to him. Because of that, everyone at my old hospital questioned me and my abilities. When the whole world thought you were incompetent, it was hard not to believe them.

I took a deep breath. This was Brooke, my friend. Not a patient. I headed for the front room and took stock of her face. She had good color, and her eyes were calm.

I knelt next to the couch. "How long has this been going on?"

"All afternoon. I didn't think much of it while I was at work, but then I couldn't walk when it happened, and I panicked. I'm sorry I ruined your night." Her eyes welled up with tears, and she swallowed heavily.

"Forget about it. There wasn't anything to ruin." I lied right through my teeth for her. The small amount of peace I'd been able to gather on the deck had flown away the moment she'd called. That was okay. I'd take one for my friend any day.

Her face pinched.

I felt her belly. It was hard, like all the muscles had cramped. "Does it hurt?" Contractions, though typically painful for most people, could be very different for others. Some women had them in their back, while others experienced only mild discomfort. I'd seen and worked with all types of deliveries.

"No, it's just tight and uncomfortable."

I started a stopwatch on my phone and leaned back against the couch. It was a waiting game now. I wasn't going to check her for progress unless we had more symptoms pop up. For now, being calm was the best thing I could do for my friend, even if I was freaking out inside.

Brooke shoved my arm. "Tell me about Dr. Dangerous—it'll keep my mind off things."

"The cabin is pretty. Totally what you'd think of when someone says 'cabin.' Braided rugs on the floor, overstuffed leather furniture that's been worn with time and use. A porch that looks out over the lake. It was nice." I paused, mentally going back to the view. "The leaves are changing, so the trees were stunning."

"Sounds like a great house, but that's not what I meant. How was the doctor? Tell me about him." She grinned like a cat with cream as she settled deeper into the cushions.

I hated and loved how she perked up at the idea of talking about Carter. I loved it because it meant she was not as worried about her baby. I hated it because it did nothing to help me sort out my confused feelings for the man.

I pointed at her. "You're using this situation to pump me for information."

She smiled, and her belly relaxed, letting me know the contraction was over. I kept the stopwatch going to see how long we had between them. "Hey, if I'm going into early labor, I might as well get something out of it."

My smile was wooden. Early labor? The words triggered a memory.

"She's in early labor," said the admit nurse. "But I got a funny feeling something's not right."

I checked the chart. "Her blood pressure is high but within normal range. Have you done a urine test?"

"I just sent it in."

That was the beginning of the nightmare. If only the doctor had looked at the results ...

"Ellise?"

I blinked and was back in my apartment.

Brooke reached for my hand. "It's started again."

I checked my stopwatch. "I'm going to ... grab a paper so I can chart this." I ran to the kitchen, my heart pounding and my hands sweating. I couldn't do this. Normally, I had a good head on my shoulders and didn't panic, but I was completely panicking now.

At least I knew enough to know I couldn't trust myself. That was something, right? Brooke needed my help, and I was failing her.

Who could I trust with my friend and my panic attack?

Carter.

His name rose up through the haze like a beacon. I blinked a few times.

What was I thinking? Carter? Really?

My heart pounded, and I felt light-headed. Worried that I might collapse and hit my head, I pushed aside my fear and grabbed my phone. I would do anything for Brooke, even if that meant facing the man I'd just run away from. My hands shook as I dialed his number. He'd seen me fall apart in the elevator, so I wouldn't have to explain. That right there made him the best option in the world.

He answered on the first ring. "Hello?"

"Hi," I jumped in, not caring if I sounded crazy and not even attempting to filter myself. I was a glass case of emotions, and everything came tumbling out before I could stop it. "Can you do me a favor? Brooke is having some issues and the clinic is closed, and normally, I would know what to do, but I don't know what to do." Tears, hot and shameful, pricked my eyes until I finally had to shut them.

He asked a couple questions about her overall health and pain levels. I did my best to answer them, trying not to sound like a scared thirteen-year-old on her first babysitting job.

"I'm in town and on my way. Can you text me your address?"

I sniffed, loud and not all attractive. "Yes."

"Ellise—I need you to hold her hand. Are you charting?"

I glanced down at my phone where the stopwatch restarted when I hit the lap button. "Yes."

"Okay. Just keep charting and sit by her. If things get worse, call 911, okay?"

I nodded. I could do that. I could sit there and hold her hand. I'd been doing that when I had a flashback. With Carter on the way, I had a deadline. Which meant I only had to keep it together until he showed up. I could do that. "Okay."

We hung up, and I found the pad of paper that we left notes for each other on and a bottle of water; then I headed back into the living room. Gathering false bravado, I said, "You're going to love this—Carter's coming over. To check on you, not to see me."

Brooke twisted so that she was looking over her shoulder at me. Her eyes widened, and in that moment, I was grateful for Carter. Where I'd seen fear in her gaze earlier, it was now replaced with unsaid teases. "Sure, *that's* why he's coming." She took the water bottle I handed her and drank deeply.

I settled back down on the floor and patted her hand. "He likes you. He told me."

"Well, he has great taste." She laid her head back and took another long chug from the water bottle.

I started writing down what I knew. The process helped clear my mind and allowed me to focus. Brooke seemed calm, and that helped me be calm.

"Can I eat yet? I'm starving." She rubbed her belly distractedly.

"As soon as you get the clearance from the doctor."

Right on cue, there were three solid knocks on the front door. I blew out my breath as I moved to stand.

"Thanks for coming," I said as I opened the door. I stopped short at the beautiful woman standing beside him. A pit formed in my stomach as my gaze raked over her long, thin frame and stunning hair. Not a piece of it was out of place, and she had a confidence about her that I envied. Who was this?

"This is my sister, Penny. She's a nurse." Carter pushed past me, not waiting for an invite inside, and headed right for the couch. He carried a black bag, like they used to have on television shows. Only this one was made of nylon instead of leather. The sight of it brought me comfort; it made me feel like Carter was better equipped to handle anything Brooke could throw at him right now.

Penny patted my back as she came inside. "It's going to be okay."

Relief filled my body, though I wasn't sure if it was relief that Penny was a medical professional or because she was his sister. I'd have to look closer at that feeling later on. Right now, Brooke was our priority. "It's nice to meet you," I said.

Carter had taken up my spot on the floor and was giving Brooke a preliminary exam as he pressed his fingers to her wrist and asked her questions. Penny set to work taking her blood pressure.

The soft *whoosh-whoosh* of the cuff hit me like a gale-force wind, and I grabbed the back of the couch to steady myself.

Penny looked up, and her eyes grew wide. She left Brooke and came around to me, helping me into a chair. I moved like my legs were not my own.

"Have a seat." She took the cuff off Brooke and put it on me. "Your blood pressure is elevated." She let out the air in the cuff and removed her stethoscope from her ears.

"I feel light-headed." I leaned over and put my head between my knees, not caring who saw or how they felt about it—or about me. Okay, I did care a little that Carter was watching me fall apart—*again*. The guy had so much going for him, and I kept fainting in his presence. Maybe I could convince him that he was the one causing fainting spells. Guys ate that stuff up, didn't they?

The next thing I knew, Carter's firm hands found my cheeks and lifted my head. He had crouched down in front of me with my face between his hands, and he was staring into my eyes. My heart thrummed as I took the color of his irises. He had amazing eyes, the kind that were a window to the soul. Everyone's eyes were supposed to be like that, but they weren't. Most people were closed off—not Carter.

"It's okay, Ellise. Brooke's okay," he said softly. His voice reminded me of the chocolate he'd given me earlier. Smooth and deep.

Not wanting him to stare into my soul anymore, I turned my gaze on my friend, who was wiggling her way to sitting.

Penny came in, carrying a plate with a sandwich, and handed it to Brooke. "She can eat. Braxton-Hicks are uncomfortable, but they aren't a danger to her or the baby."

"I know," I answered softly as my body began to relax. I knew what Braxton-Hicks were. But that didn't mean they weren't frightening.

Carter cocked his head, and I dropped my gaze to keep my secrets at bay.

Instead, I focused on what Penny had said. *Braxton-Hicks. Nonthreatening. Totally normal. It's going to be okay,* I chanted in my mind.

"She's dehydrated," I said out of habit.

Carter nodded. "Probably."

I smiled. "I gave her some water."

"You did good." He patted my knee. "A part of you must have known what she needed."

I sat all the way up, wondering if that were true. Had my training and instincts worked even while I was freaking out? That was ... comforting. I took a deep breath, and the anxious clouds began to clear. I'd done the right thing. I'd helped my friend, and I'd gotten a doctor here. Yes, I almost fainted, but that hadn't been my first reaction.

"Thank you for coming." I placed my hand over his on my knee. It was a seemingly innocent gesture, but suddenly, heat began to crawl across my skin from where we touched.

My breath caught in my throat when he didn't move to pull away. Instead, he smiled at me as if he weren't in the least bit affected. "Anytime."

"You know," Penny interjected. "She really should be monitored overnight. Normally, I'd volunteer, but ..." She looked at Carter, something in her eyes saying there was more that she didn't want to say out loud.

Carter pushed to his feet. "What do you suggest?" he asked as he cradled his chin in his hand. I could see that he was appeasing his sister's overprotectiveness of Brooke, and it was adorable.

Penny pressed her lips together, glanced at me, and then focused on Carter.

Even though she didn't intend for it to happen, that glance made me feel small. I hadn't told anyone in town about what had happened, and Carter was only piecing things together from what he'd seen. Maybe I could tell him, but then ... well, what if he looked at me differently? Like the doctors at my old hospital did—with pity, and in one case, disgust. They thought that I couldn't cut it. Did I want him to feel the same?

I pushed to my feet, willing my legs to stay solid and hold me up. They did a pretty good job, so I continued. "We're fine. Really."

Brooke nodded. "I'm feeling much better." She held up her almost empty water bottle. "In fact, I need to make a pit stop."

Carter offered a hand to help her up, and she waddled to the bathroom.

"See? Much better," I said, suddenly wanting Penny's support of my conclusion. The fact that Carter brought Penny along meant he trusted her opinion. I liked that about him, liked that he trusted a nurse, relied on her, even. Lots of doctors didn't listen to us nurses. I paused my train of thought right there. That was the first time I'd thought of myself as a nurse in a while. It was strange and yet right. I shook my train of thought to start chugging. Dwelling on semantics wasn't going to get me anywhere.

Penny smiled. "I'd feel better if Carter were here."

My train let out a warning whistle. "Wait. Overnight? Here?" I pointed to the carpet. "In my apartment?"

"Pen," Carter said as he leaned closer to her. Some sort of unspoken sibling dialogue went on between them. The words were lost on me, but the meaning wasn't. Carter's eyes were exceptionally wide as he stared her down. He wasn't going to push staying here.

But Penny was a formidable force and wasn't budging. Perhaps she was the older sister? Instead, she turned to smile at me. "You can come sleep at my parents' if you're uncomfortable with Carter," offered Penny. "We have lots of room."

"No." The answer was automatic. I wasn't going to leave my friend. And it wasn't that I was uncomfortable with Carter here to watch over her. I was uncomfortable with the feelings Carter stirred inside of me.

"I don't have to stay here. I don't want to make you uncomfortable." Carter gave me a sympathetic smile.

I studied him, a war going on inside of my mind. On the one side was reason, which stated that having a doctor on call all night would be a huge help. On the other, this was *Carter*, the man who made butterflies twirl in my stomach and heated my body with a touch.

Then, I remembered the fear in Brooke's voice when she'd called me and the panic on her expression when I'd walked into the apartment. The more I thought about it, the more I realized that I didn't have a reason to feel weird about this. Carter was here to keep an eye on Brooke, and I was her roommate. End of story.

I took in a deep breath and said, "I'll find some sheets for the couch."

Penny pinched her lips together and nodded as Carter smiled. "That'll work. Thanks."

I turned, but not before I caught the grateful look Carter gave Penny and her wink in return.

Oh well. It didn't matter if they were conspiring to get Carter on my couch or not. I knew Brooke would feel better knowing that he was there. And she was all that mattered to me.

Even if his presence left me feeling like the world had tipped sideways, it was still nice to know that I wasn't going to be alone. And for someone who'd been running from her past, *alone* was becoming my middle name.

I made it to the hall closet and began digging for our extra set of sheets. A very pesky thought entered my mind. What if there was more to Dr. Dangerous than his good looks? What if he was the kind of guy a girl could lean on?

I shook those questions loose as I pulled out the sheet set. He was dangerous because he was getting past my walls, and I didn't like that one bit. If I was going to survive my time here in Evergreen Hollow, I needed to forget the doctor now laughing and joking with Brooke.

I needed to forget him like my life depended on it. Period.

CHAPTER SEVEN
CARTER

For a couch, the one that Ellise had me sleep on was … awful.

It looked harmless enough, until I found the hard and pokey springs that jabbed into my lower back like I'd offended their grandma or something.

I spent most of the night tossing and turning in an attempt to find a comfortable spot. No amount of punching the cushions or adjusting the pillows helped. Instead, I lay there, attempting to sleep while no heavy Zs came.

I couldn't stop thinking about Ellise. Her room was right there, the door firmly shut against me—not that I'd try and sneak in to watch her sleep. That would be creepy. It would be nice to know someone was getting some shut-eye, though.

I didn't have to wonder about Brooke. She snored—loudly.

It was possible that Ellise shut her door against Brooke's chainsaw and not against me.

A guy could hope.

And he could take weird tangents in the middle of the night when he didn't have a way to distract himself.

My phone was almost dead, and the charger was in the car. I didn't want to wake the house by opening and closing the front door. So I lay there, staring at the ceiling and making a mortal enemy out of the couch.

When the sun started to peek through the half-drawn drapes on the far wall, I sighed and threw the comforter off my body, wishing I could throw off the whole sleepless night as easily. I scrubbed my face a few times, hoping to rub some life into my skin. I could go 72 hours without sleep and still function—a skill honed in med school. Still, I didn't want to look like a grizzly who hadn't gotten his winter nap. I settled my feet on the floor and stood.

I needed a shower. I grabbed my overnight bag from by the door. As a doctor, I always had one handy.

I padded into the bathroom that sat between Brooke's and Ellise's rooms and shut the door. I needed some warm water on my face if I was going to have a hope and a prayer of waking up.

After the bathroom was good and steamy and I felt human again, I turned off the shower, grabbed a nearby towel, and wrapped it around my waist. I pulled open the curtain and was met with an earsplitting scream.

Ellise stood near the toilet with her thumbs hooked on the top of her kitten-covered pajama bottoms. She looked half awake and scared to death as she stared at me. Her normally perfect hair was tousled, and her eyes were bigger than the moon that had kept me company all night long.

Realizing what she was about to do, she straightened and pulled her hands free. She went to run her hand through her hair, only to have it catch in the knots. She swallowed. "What are you doing in here?"

Her gaze slipped down to my chest, and I couldn't help but smile at her attempt to keep it level with my eyes. I wasn't as big as my brother Mason, who trained in the Army Rangers, but I wasn't a scrawny kid either. Knowing how to work all my angles, I folded my arms across my chest, making sure that my muscles flexed in the process. She squirmed, and I did a mental fist pump.

"Is this how you treat all of your guests?" I asked as she moved to push her hair from her reddened face.

"I—what?" she asked, completely avoiding meeting my gaze. The room was steamy and hot.

"Your guests. Do you normally barge in on their showers?" I reached up and pushed my hand through my hair, causing droplets of water to spray around me.

Ellise made a noise that sounded like a stifled gasp, which did crazy things to my ego. Right now, I had all her attention, and I was going to revel in it as long as I could.

"I thought you were Brooke. We share a bathroom, which means we go pee—" She pinched her lips as her skin flushed more. "Never mind. I'm going back to bed."

I chuckled as I swung a leg over the tub and stepped out onto the bath mat, bringing our bodies—and therefore my bare chest—within inches of each other. The bathroom was small enough that it barely held us both. She stiffened and attempted to back up away from me. My grin deepened of its own accord. She was all flustered, and the look was so hot on her.

"Don't let me chase you off." I gestured to the shower. "You can hop in. I'll even let you borrow my towel." I put a hand to the spot where I'd tucked in a corner.

Ellise looked from me to the shower stall and back to me. "I, um …" If she were a robot, she would short-circuit right now.

If I didn't back off, I feared she'd overheat. Not to mention my thoughts weren't all PG after mentioning she could jump in the shower. Jeez, I should have picked my words a little better. I backpedaled. "Joking. I'll go change in your room while you pee." I grabbed my overnight bag and pulled the strap over my bare shoulder.

"That's, um, that's okay," she called after me. "You can stay here, and I'll go back to my room."

I waved her comment away. She mumbled something under her breath and then shut the bathroom door. Now alone, I glanced around her room. It was small but tidy. The blankets were bright colors, teal blues and hot pinks that said she was more fun than she liked to let on. There was a picture on her nightstand of her family at the Grand Canyon. It couldn't have been taken that long ago. I looked closer. Her hair had been shorter then.

Either she had just moved here, or she was a minimalist. Besides her clothes and a few trinkets on her dresser, she had nothing else in the room.

The sparsity of everything made me wonder more about her than they answered any questions I had. Was she trying to find herself again? Or had she just lost her way and needed to get back on the path God intended her to walk? Was that in the medical field? Had she been put in my path for another reason, one that included future showers together as husband and wife?

Whoa! I put on the mental brakes. Another side effect of not sleeping was that my thoughts drifted too far afield and I became philosophical. My brothers said I'd been horrible company at sleepovers when we were kids.

I dressed quickly and used the towel to dry off my hair. After running some gel through it so it looked mussed but not too styled, I pulled open the door to find Ellise leaning against the wall beside the door, chewing on her thumbnail. She looked concerned.

"I didn't steal anything. You can search me if you want." I raised both hands. Hopefully, she'd remember what was under the Henley.

Bingo! Her cheeks flushed, and she didn't meet my gaze as she slipped into her room and shut the door.

I chuckled as I stood in the hallway, wondering if I'd pushed her too far. It wasn't like I'd barged in on her in the bathroom. I thought the tally went two for her and zero for me in this department. She'd seen my bare chest twice. That meant some teasing was in order, right?

Before I lost myself staring at her door and wondering if she found me as adorable as I found myself this morning, I moved to the living room, where I set my bag next to the door, and then headed into the kitchen. It was about a tenth the size of my parents' kitchen, but it was clean and I was hungry. Knowing pregnant women, Brooke was going to be hungry when she got up too.

I located some bread and eggs and decided my to-die-for French toast was in order. After I acquainted myself with the spice cupboard, the air in the apartment began to smell of cinnamon and vanilla. My mouth watered as I slipped a corner of the cooked toast into my mouth.

"This is so not fair." A voice startled me, and I whipped around to see Brooke standing there. She wore a pair of maternity pajamas and a scowl. She had her arms crossed, and she was eyeing me as if I were a renegade in her kitchen and not the sheriff of French toast I was trying to be.

I plated a few slices. "What's not fair?"

She slipped onto a barstool next to the peninsula. "I should be sleeping, but these smells literally beckoned me from my bed." She waved her hand through the air as if sampling the scents.

I grabbed the warmed maple syrup and set it next to the plate I'd placed in front of her. Mom had taught me well.

Brooke's eyes widened as I handed her a fork. "For me?"

I nodded. "I know pregnant women. You feed them first if you want to live."

Brooke laughed, but she didn't wait for me to finish speaking before she got busy drizzling syrup on the toast. She took a bite, let out a soft moan while closing her eyes, and then raised her fork and waggled it in my direction. "I had a feeling about you."

I chuckled as I returned to dipping bread in the egg mixture. My eyes cut to Ellise's door—still shut. I wondered how long it would take for her to venture out for food. "I hope it was a good feeling."

She snorted, and when I peeked over my shoulder, she was almost done with the two pieces of toast I'd given her to start. I gathered two more up on my spatula and set them on her plate.

She groaned and nodded. "Yep. It was a good feeling."

"Because I feed you?" I didn't know why I cared so much, except this was Ellise's best friend—the person who knew more about her than any other in town. I knew one thing about women: if the best friend liked you, you were in. Thank you, *Hitch*, for teaching me that tidbit.

Once Brooke finished chewing a forkful, she moved to study me. "I always welcome people who want to feed me, but that's not what I had a good feeling about. I just ... like you." She gave me a wink, and for a moment, I feared what she meant by that.

How could I reject a pregnant woman? "I, um ..." My brain coughed and sputtered, and all of Mom's lessons on how a man should treat a woman came rushing back to me.

Be kind.

Tell her she's beautiful.

Act as if you care—even if you don't, you blockhead.

I set a cup of milk in front of her and backed away—keeping the appropriate distance between us.

Brooke must have noticed my brain spasm, because she snorted and shook her head. "Not like that." Then she began to laugh. "You are so not my type."

I was relieved but a bit offended by how hard she laughed. I wasn't a slab of day-old bologna or anything. "Ouch."

Brooke took a sip of milk. "Don't be offended. Trust me, this is a box you want to keep shut." She eyed me over her glass as she took another drink. "But Ellise ..." she said slowly as she lowered her glass to the counter.

My ears perked up. But I didn't want to seem too eager, so I returned to the pan and removed the four pieces of toast that were finishing up. I held them up for Brooke, but she shook her head. "I'm stuffed."

I nodded and plated them for myself and Ellise. She had to come out sometime, right? I dove in. I secretly hoped that Brooke would continue with her discussion of Ellise without my prodding. I wanted to know more about this mysterious woman without it seeming like I wanted to know. It was a guy thing. Women would ask questions and go back and forth for hours. We guys, we wanted to know it all; we just didn't want to *look* like we wanted to know it all.

Thankfully, Brooke didn't need any encouragement to steer her back to Ellise. She got there on her own, and I was left to lean against the counter with my legs extended, listening while I ate.

She told me that she and Ellise had grown up together. She talked about how outgoing Ellise had been in high school and how shy she'd been. They'd been yin and yang yet managed to find a friendship amongst their differences. Or maybe because of them.

She grew quieter as she discussed college, graduation, and life after, when they'd set out to conquer the world and then ... didn't.

Her cheeks flushed, and she pinched her lips together. "You can see where my life went." She pointed to her stomach. "But Ellise was a rising star. She had it all going for her until—well, that's her story to tell."

I was finished with my food, so I moved to the sink to rinse my dish. I wanted—no, needed—to know more about the things Ellise faced every day, and I feared that she would never be open enough to tell me.

The other side of that coin was if I waited too long to ask, she'd pull away and I'd be left with nothing. "She must have gone through something terrible," I prodded as I shook the water off the dish and loaded it into the dishwasher.

"Yeah."

When Brooke didn't offer more, I took her plate from her and started rinsing it. Sometimes, with patients, I waited out their thinking process and they were able to give me more information. Silence was a good motivator.

"It's really something you should hear from her." Brooke sighed, shaking her head. "Besides, I would most likely mess up the medical jargon for what happened."

I stilled, digesting what she'd unintentionally revealed in her statement. So whatever had happened, it had happened at work. I'd had a feeling Ellise was a L&D nurse. Not just from her reaction in the elevator when listening to the two nurses talk, but from the way her brain had connected dots last night about Brooke being dehydrated and such.

Her trauma most likely came from the death of either a mom or the baby.

My heart broke for Ellise.

I'd lost a handful of patients myself. It took a toll on the spirit and one's soul to have that happen. We weren't robots or computer programs. We had hearts, and they suffered right along with our patients and their families.

I wished I could take away her pain and help her see the other side of this. As medical professionals, we only had so much control. The rest was left up to God. It was a truth I'd learned early on in my medical career, and it had helped me many times.

"Anyway, deep stuff," Brooke said as she took her now-rinsed plate from me and loaded it into the dishwasher. After the soap was added, she leaned against the counter and folded her arms. "So what are your intentions with Ellise?"

Her question threw me off guard, and I paused, my lips open but unable to form any words. I cleared my throat. "My intentions?" I finally asked. I'd had all kinds of thoughts that morning ranging from showing off in front of the flustered woman to tangents that ended with rings and vows.

She nodded. "With my best friend. As her only family around and her spiritual guide, I need to know what you have planned for her."

I raised my eyebrows. I wasn't sure what to say to that. A lot of what I wanted had to do with Ellise and what she wanted. Did she want *me*? "I, um …" I pushed my hand through my hair, unwilling to show my cards first. I liked her. I felt compelled to protect her and help her out. Did I want more? Kind of … Okay, yes. I didn't want to leave the apartment today and not have a return date.

Which was big for me, considering the whole Holly thing. Hmm, maybe I was more over her than I'd thought even a couple days ago. It was possible that it took the right woman to bump me out of the hole Holly had dumped me in. I pressed my hand to my head. I really needed sleep, because I was getting way too deep into my thoughts.

Brooke laughed and swatted my arm. "Let's start with today. Will that work better?"

I blew out my breath and nodded. "I can handle today."

Brooke raised her eyebrows. "Then what's your plan for today, Dr. Dangerous?"

I studied her, mulling her question around in my mind. The nickname didn't bother me anymore; these two were quirky that way, and they'd given me a glimpse behind the curtain. Which I appreciated.

I was free from work, but I wasn't sure if Ellise was off today. The thought of spending the day with her caused excitement to rise inside of me. I wondered if I should just lean into it, like wakeboarding, where you came up against the wake and let the board pull you over. "It would be nice to spend some time with her," I said slowly, and as noncommittally as possible. Another guy trait I possessed, I suppose.

Brooke nodded with each word, and her smile grew wider as I finished. Then she punched my shoulder and grinned. "I think that's perfect."

"What's perfect?"

We both turned to see Ellise standing in the living room. Her hair was damp, and she was dressed in a pair of jeans and a soft white sweater. I smiled—I couldn't help it. I felt like I'd been waiting for this moment since I'd seen her twenty minutes ago, and it was finally here.

Ellise didn't look at me. Instead, she walked over to the coffee pot and filled a mug. Then she turned, leaned against the counter, and took small sips, all the while avoiding my gaze. "You're going to spend the day with Carter," Brooke said as she moved to grab a water bottle from the fridge.

I peeked over at Ellise to see that her expression had hardened. It hurt, but I tried to be understanding. I had teased her mercilessly not long ago. Where I wanted to open myself up, she had a broken past. I could respect that. The trouble was, spending the day with her would take me deeper into these feelings that grew without effort. I'd be putting myself on the line, and she might never reciprocate. It was a gamble I was willing to take, which told me I was really over Holly and ready to move on. Which felt good—darn good.

"I mean, if you want to," I hurried to add. There was nothing more demoralizing than forcing someone to spend time with you.

"No, no." Brooke held her hand out. "She needs this." Then she turned to focus on Ellise. "You need this." Her tone brokered no arguments.

Ellise studied Brooke before glancing up at me, uncertainty in her gaze. She was battling within herself for a moment. Then she sighed. "Fine."

Brooke clapped her hands

"Only if Brooke comes with," Ellise hurried to add.

Brooke's excitement died down as she pinched her lips and glanced up at me. Then she shrugged. "You want a big pregnant woman messing with your groove, Dr. D.?"

Ellise linked arms with her and then turned to face me. "If I go, Brooke comes with me."

I chuckled. It was funny that she seemed to think this was a bad thing. "I get to escort two beautiful women? I think I can handle that." I took some satisfaction in the fact that Ellise's cheeks flushed. The result only made me want to compliment her more.

Brooke patted Ellise's hand. "All right, we're in, then."

I grinned as I shoved my hands into my front pockets. "So, any requests?"

CHAPTER EIGHT
ELLISE

"You know, I didn't think you'd actually take me up on this idea." Inside, I was suppressing eight-year-old Ellise, who was dying to take off through the crowd to try everything at the fair. Instead, I settled on spinning in a slow circle as I took in the crowds of people, some of them carrying stuffed animals or scarecrows that they'd won at ring toss or from fooling the "guess your weight" guy. I shook my head, making a metal note to steer clear of that booth. Seriously, who would want to do that?

Carter had a handful of tickets and a wicked grin. "This is so brilliant, I thought it was my idea."

Brooke snorted a laugh. "Listen, I smell deep-fried pickles. If you all can get along for the next ten minutes, I'm getting in a food line."

Carter handed her a line of tickets. "These work at the food booths too."

"Smart man—he's a smart man, Ellise," Brooke said as she took the tickets and held them directly under my nose.

I rolled my eyes. "He's a doctor—his intelligence isn't in question."

She wiggled her fingers and left us standing by the Ferris wheel. Silence fell around us, and suddenly, I was acutely aware of how close Carter was to me.

If he noticed, he didn't move to say anything. Instead, he lifted the tickets. "The fair is your oyster. What'll it be? The dunk tank? The corn maze? What about a churro?"

I took a second to consider my options. "Let's do some rides while Brooke is occupied. I'd feel bad making her stand at the exit while we had a good time."

"You're having a good time, then?" His eyes were alight with hope and more than a little bit of teasing. That was one thing I'd learned about him that morning: he was a tease. A horrible tease who walked around with his shirt off and flexed until my mouth was dry and my brain scrambled like an egg.

I didn't need those images in my mind, and yet I couldn't seem to get them out. Every time I looked at his square jaw, I flashed back to the moment when a single water droplet had run down his skin.

"Stop," I hissed under my breath before I could stop myself. My cheeks flushed, and I glanced up to see that Carter's smile had faltered. Feeling like an idiot, I hurried to add, "That wasn't for you."

Carter furrowed his brow. "It wasn't?" And then he glanced around while leaning into me. "Who was it for?"

Needing to redeem myself from the idiot I was slowly becoming, I waved to a man who had just passed by. "Him."

"Him?"

I nodded, desperate to move on. "Yes. Him. He was … picking his nose."

A disgusted look passed over Carter's face. I nodded, grateful that my answer seemed good enough to distract Carter. Right now, having a conversation about how I couldn't forget Carter's chest was not on my to-do list. If I was going to survive today, I needed to keep my internal thoughts to myself.

"Anyway," I said as I swung my arms to the front and back, hoping that made me look relaxed and not like a psycho. "I'm considering that I might be having a good time."

Carter paused before he chuckled. "You are so full of compliments—it's hard to be around you without blushing."

I smacked his arm. Which was a bad sign, because I did it without thinking. I just reacted. Now, I may not be a doctor, but it didn't take PhD-level intelligence to know that when a girl smacked a guy's arm, she was into him.

So, crap. I guessed I was kind of into Carter. Hopefully, I'd been the only one who'd picked up on that little fact. The last thing I needed was for him to start wondering.

"The Tilt-A-Whirl?" He pointed to the machine that literally scrambled people like eggs. It seemed fitting for my current brain situation, so I agreed.

The line wasn't too long, and we were on and laughing our guts out within two minutes. As the ride picked up speed, it threw me into Carter. My whole side was pressed up against him, and I couldn't have pulled away if I tried. When the ride stopped and we peeled ourselves from the hard bench, we shakily walked away, and I was doing everything I could to keep from falling into him. Clinging to him while on a ride was explainable. Falling into him and using him for support out in the open world was too confusing. And the last thing I needed was confusion.

"Dr. McKnight," called a woman with three kids trailing behind her. "It's so good to see you again. How's your sister? We were so excited to hear about her wedding."

Carter shuffled his feet. "Penny's doing great. Thank you for asking. Have a great time at the fair." He took my arm, gentle but insistent, and ushered us away.

"Who was that?" I couldn't help but look over my shoulder at the woman, who handed out tickets to her children. She was not following Carter's every move, so I gathered she wasn't competition.

"One of my mom's friends. They belong to the same quilting group or something."

"Oh—that's nice. Do you quilt?" I couldn't help the teasing tone in my voice.

He stopped and looked at me. "No. Why?"

"I just wondered what you do when you're not at the hospital." I lifted a shoulder as if it weren't a big deal.

He continued walking to our next ride—the screamer. Carter was stopped twice more by friends of the family.

I was ready for the roller coaster. I wasn't ready for all the attention he garnered. Seemed like everyone knew his name.

I couldn't help but feel as if Carter felt more agitated by the conversations than me. He'd picked up speed, and I had to hurry to sidestep three kids who had stumbled off the ride and looked green around the gills.

"I fish at the cabin." Carter finally answered my question when we reached the end of the line and stopped. "That's for sanity and must be duly recognized as the greatest sport known to mankind."

I leaned against the metal railing for support. "*Pft*—maybe *man*kind."

Carter squinted as he looked down at me and then up to the trees that were rustling above us. "Oh? What would womankind's greatest sport be?"

"Something a lot harder than putting a worm on a hook." I shrugged, enjoying the banter between us. Talking to him was so … easy. It relaxed me in a way that I hadn't relaxed in a long time.

"Hey now, it's not about the worm. It's about outthinking a fish."

I laughed. "That sounds so much tougher. You know, when you think about the size of a fish's brain."

The line moved, so we moved with it. After taking our new place, Carter leaned against one metal rail, and I leaned against the one across from him. The people in front of us nodded in greeting.

"So your hobby is … roller coaster junkie?" Carter asked.

I flexed my arms as if they were in any way scary. "I'm down with any roller coaster, any day. Bring it." I tapped his leg with my foot. Ugh! I had to stop finding ways to touch him. This was getting out of hand. "But I'm also in love with a good book and could spend hours curled up on a couch."

"Not your couch, I hope." He touched his lower back.

I winced. "Was it bad? I haven't actually spent a night on it."

"I've slept on worse … at scout camp … without a tent."

"I'm so sorry." I leaned forward and put my hand on his arm. He looked down, and I snatched it away, mumbling "sorry" again.

"Dr. McKnight! How are you?" asked a middle-aged man with thinning hair as he stopped to shake hands with Carter. "How's your dad? I haven't seen him on the course lately."

"He's training someone new, I think. He should be able to get out at least one more time before the end of the season."

"We're almost there now." The guy rubbed his arms as if that signified the time of year. "It was good to see you."

"You too."

All of this attention was overwhelming for me. A doctor in the limelight, who pumped hands like he was running for office, had been one of the leading factors in me leaving my last hospital. After all, who was going to listen to a lowly nurse when it was her word against that of a well-liked, well-known doctor? I lifted my eyebrows at Carter, and my stomach soured. "You know, I'm not really feeling the screamer anymore." I ducked under the rail and headed for a bench. Carter stuck with me and sat down.

I appreciated him following me, but I wasn't exactly sure what to say, and the silence stretched between us like warm taffy on a summer's day. Instead, I located my phone and texted Brooke our new location. She texted back a bunch of jumbled words, but the gist was that she had lots of food and was heading our way. I could only imagine how many different items she had tucked under her arms and in her hands.

"Did I do something wrong?" Carter asked, leaning forward to rest his elbows on his knees.

I glanced over at him and sighed. "It's not you."

"Please—I don't need that speech this week." He leaned back and gave me a pointed look. "*It's not you, it's me?*" he asked.

Why did it sound like we were breaking up? We weren't anything. Did he ... I shook my head slightly as I forced those thoughts from my mind. I was truly crazy.

Not wanting to give him the wrong idea, I gave him a half-hearted smile as I took in a deep breath. "The thing is ..." I pinched my lips together. How much did I want to tell him? How far was I willing to let him in? I wasn't quite sure. And then, the desire to open up washed over me, and I decided to lean into it. I wanted to trust Carter. It was a strange sensation, and yet it felt as natural as breathing.

"There was this doctor at my old hospital—a town favorite. Anyway, we had a—" What would I even call it? I settled on using the term they'd placed in my file. "*Misunderstanding*. I thought he made the wrong call. He blamed me. It was my word against his, and he was the one with all the friends, the reputation, the clout. So I was the one who had to move on." I lifted a shoulder as if it didn't matter, but it did. It mattered a whole lot. Enough that even now, I teared up.

Feeling stupid and emotional, I swiped at my cheeks and surged to my feet. Anxiety flooded my veins. All I wanted was to get away from this moment and the feelings that threatened to overtake me.

Carter jumped up and hooked my elbow, stopping me and turning me in to his chest. I stiffened but then slowly began to relax. I mean, I was broken, but I was also a woman. Every part of his body was meant to be next to mine. Out of instinct, I'd sprawled my hands across his pecks when he'd swung me into his body, and the desire to withdraw disappeared when I took in his wonderfully solid chest. It was the kind of body a woman could fall asleep against, and I was exhausted. He wrapped his arms around me and held me there, letting me tremble until I settled.

"What happened to you isn't right."

"Carter—"

"Give me his name. I'll have him removed from practice."

I wasn't sure what Brooke had told him, but it sounded like he'd pieced together a few things. I knew he was smart. "It's not that easy. Like I said, he's Dr. Perfect, and no one believes that he made a mistake."

"I believe you." His voice was deep and calm—warm, even.

"Thanks. You and Brooke are the only ones."

He pulled back to study me. Then, he reached up to brush his knuckles over my cheek. My entire body responded despite my efforts to keep myself at bay as I leaned in.

"What can I do?" he asked, his voice low and throaty.

I shook my head quickly. "There's nothing to do. I just have to find a way to move on."

He cupped my face, staring deeply into my eyes. "Is there any way that you could trust me to help?"

I swallowed. "There's a big question." I stepped away, effectively breaking our hug. I took in a deep breath as I fiddled with the strap of my purse.

"Even Dr. Dangerous can be a good guy." Carter's voice was low, and I couldn't help but sense the teasing in his tone.

I burst out laughing. I needed to release some of this tension that had built up between us. "I'm going to kill Brooke. She told you that nickname, didn't she? Did she tell you about Dr. Disaster too?"

His mouth fell open. "When did I earn that one?"

"When you knocked my pot on the ground."

He opened his mouth like he was going to put the blame back on me—teasingly, of course—but stopped. I appreciated his sensitivity. Maybe I could trust him, just enough to let him in a little. And letting him in didn't mean I was handing him my heart. I needed to remember that.

Our laughter died down, and I couldn't help but warm under Carter's smile. He looked relaxed as he settled back down onto the bench with his arm slung haphazardly across the back. He leaned forward and patted his hand on the seat next to him.

Despite all my reservations, I moved to sit. Then, feeling brave, I took in a deep breath and turned to face him. His brilliant blue eyes cut through my fears, and for the first time, I felt the desire to trust: trust him, trust this town, trust the new life I was trying to find here.

"Okay," I said softly.

He furrowed his brow and repeated, "Okay?"

I nodded. "Okay. I'm willing to give you a try."

He studied me and then dropped his arm so he could rest both elbows on his knees. "You're going to trust me?"

"Yes." Fear clung to me, and I so desperately wanted to run away, but I couldn't. Not when the pull to Carter was this strong. I bit my lip and studied my shoes. Trusting didn't come easy—probably because I didn't trust myself.

I hoped that would work itself out, and soon. If it didn't, I wouldn't be in any shape to see this relationship go anywhere, and I'd be on the road again, looking for a new place and a new chance.

CHAPTER NINE
CARTER

Something had shifted in Ellise. She seemed so small. So vulnerable. And so not the woman who'd I run into with the spaghetti sauce. For the first time since I'd met her, I'd seen just how broken she was. Because it wasn't just about her ability to work as a nurse. Whatever trauma she'd been through had broken her faith in mankind. Which was a shame, because the world deserved to see her smile, hear her laugh, and share in her light. She had so much light inside, but it was muted. And now, more than ever, I wanted to help her fix whatever was ailing her and shine bright again.

No matter what.

But before I could open my heart up and tell her all the feelings building inside of me, Brooke waddled up to us with her arms, hands, and mouth completely full of all sorts of fair food. I smiled and helped her unload her goodies, setting them carefully on the bench and the rim of the planter next to us. I caught whiffs of chocolate, popcorn, caramel, and something spicy that I wasn't sure would go well with the other flavors.

"Ooh, mini doughnuts, please," Ellise said as she reached out her hands and wiggled her fingers.

Brooke swatted her hand away. "You don't take food from a

pregnant lady." Even though her tone was sweet, her warning was not lost on me. From the look on Ellise's face, it wasn't lost on her either.

"Geez," Ellise said as she emphatically shook her hand out and then blew on it a few times.

I chuckled at their antics as I stood in the background, watching these two converse. It made me think of my siblings. We'd fight and pick on each other, but when it came down to being there for one another, that was a given. We'd do anything for the one who was struggling.

And right now, from what I could tell, both of these women were struggling.

Time seemed to speed by as we hung out. Brooke and Ellise had their inside jokes and occasionally let me in on some of them. Any other time, I would have felt out of place as they giggled and ate, but for some odd reason, I didn't feel that way at all. If anything, I felt at home. A feeling only reserved for my parents' house.

My two-bedroom apartment next to the hospital wasn't my home. It was a place where I stayed between shifts. Mom and Dad's place spoke to a simpler time for me, when people's lives weren't in my hands and all I had to worry about was where I spent Friday night or my biology grade. The pressure to be a McKnight was always there, but in the home, it was coupled with a whole lot of love and acceptance.

So it was strange that standing here, listening to these two women laugh and joke, gave me that same sense of satisfaction. Maybe I needed to pay Dr. Thornbush a visit up in the psych ward to get my head examined.

"Well, well, well. Look who had a party and didn't invite me." Grant clamped a hand down on my shoulder and squeezed.

I laughed easily. He wasn't the type to get offended. "I don't need the competition." I elbowed him. Even though I was joking, he was a smooth talker, and I didn't want to see him put the moves on Ellise. Not that he stood a chance. She was much too inside of herself to respond to Grant's brazen flirting.

"I can see what you're worried about. Ladies, it's pleasure to see you both again." He held out his hand. Brooke slipped hers into it, and he pressed a kiss to her skin, maintaining eye contact all the while. Brooke blushed and pulled her hand back quickly.

Ellise offered a wave, not even letting him close to her. See? Smart woman. I felt an odd sense of manly pride knowing that she'd let me closer than she let Grant.

Brooke threw the popcorn container in the nearby trash. "I think I've had enough festivities for the day." She let out a big sigh and moved to stand. Grant was right there, holding her arm and steadying her. It took a few times for her to navigate her belly and straighten.

I was in shock at my buddy's chivalry. It wasn't that he was a jerk. He was always polite. It was just that he liked playing the field. Flirting was a sport, like a pick-up game of basketball between shifts. He was good at it too, and the way he held Brooke's arm had nothing to do with flirting.

"You're going home?" Ellise asked.

I tried to ignore the sense of disappointment in her voice.

Brooke motioned toward her feet. "If I'm on these puppies any longer, I'm going to float out of here." Her ankles looked swollen, and for a moment, I allowed the doctor side of me to surface.

"Have you talked to your doctor about them?" I knelt down in front of her and reached out to touch her ankles, only to have her grab my hand and attempt to pull me up.

"Oh no. No, I'm not your patient today." She waggled her pointer finger in my direction. "If they get worse, I'll chat with my OB. But for now, you two are going to promise me that you will stay here and have fun."

Ellise parted her lips, but before I was going to allow her to make an excuse as to why we needed to leave, I stepped between them. "Of course we will," I said as I linked arms with Ellise. "It's the least we could do for you."

I could feel Ellise's stare on me, but I didn't waver. Instead, I kept my smile focused on Brooke, who was sweeping her gaze between Ellise and me. Then a smile crept across her face as she nodded, shoved her purse farther up her shoulder, and muttered, "I'm a genius."

I wasn't sure what she was referring to, but I had a good idea. It wasn't lost on me that Brooke seemed determined for something to happen between Ellise and I. And I would be lying if there wasn't a part of me that was hoping for the same thing.

"I'll have her home by midnight," I said with a wide smile.

Brooke snorted. "If you're having fun, I'm cool with three in the morning."

"Brooke," Ellise hissed, but it was drowned out by Brooke's, Grant's, and my laughter. I heard Ellise sigh as I felt her body relax. Good, we were wearing her down.

"Do you need a ride?" asked Grant. He'd already pulled his keys out of his pocket.

"Aren't you here for the fair?" Brooke gestured toward the rides and things.

Grant shook his head. "I think I found what I came here for."

I exchanged a surprised look with Ellise.

Brooke's cheeks dusted with color, and she glanced down. "A ride would be nice."

"Your carriage awaits." Grant offered his arm, and she slipped her hand in the crook of his elbow.

"Bye, I'm outta here," Brooke said as she blew a kiss to Ellise. Then she turned and asked Grant, "Do you mind if we stop for a shake?"

"I was thinking an early dinner," Grant replied.

"Even better." Brooke beamed.

"Should I be worried about that?" Ellise asked, pointing at the two of them walking slowly toward the exit.

I concentrated on their movements. Grant wasn't trying to snuggle closer or make a move. He was all charm and smiles and proper distancing. "I don't think so. Grant is not usually this attentive to a woman. It's a whole new side of him. But I trust the guy with my life."

Ellise let out a sigh. "Then I might be able to trust him with my best friend. *Might*," she emphasized.

Now alone with Ellise, I peeked down at her to see that despite the fact that she was ignoring my gaze, she'd allowed our arms to remain linked. I wanted to convince myself that her physical affection today was all in my head, that she wasn't touching me because she wanted to, but because she hadn't thought better of it or because she was the type of girl who smacked a guy's arm every five minutes. But there was a tiny voice in the back of my mind that told me I wasn't a fool. Ellise was interested in me, even if she was the only one who didn't know it.

Not wanting to lose the magic that had sparked between us earlier, I tightened my hold on her and began weaving her through the crowds.

"Where are we going?" she asked.

I laughed as I headed toward the Ferris wheel. "You'll just have trust me."

~

Three hours later, we were exhausted yet happy. It took some time, but I eventually got her to lower her guard and be herself like she'd done earlier. There was even a point where I got her laughing uncontrollably, and it felt like I'd performed a bladder cystectomy to perfection.

She was a complicated nut to crack, but with every conversation and with every beaming smile she sent my way, she was slowly letting me in.

And it felt great.

The early evening air wafted around us, bringing the scent of roasted nuts and the hint of winter weather to come. We weren't talking, just enjoying the sounds of the rides and screams. The smell of cinnamon and fried food filled my nose, and I couldn't help but breathe in deep.

If this was what heaven was like, sign me up.

"Well, this was a—"

"Want to try a do—"

We both spoke at the same time and halted at the same time. I glanced down at Ellise, who pinched her lips and fought a smile. I chuckled as I passed through the exit turnstile and stepped back so Ellise could do the same.

"Go ahead," I said, extending my arm out.

She shook her head. "No, that's okay. You go first."

I contemplated fighting her, but I had a sinking suspicion that she wanted to call it a night, so I took charge. "I was wondering if you wanted to try the cabin once more. We could light a bonfire. Maybe pick up some Mexican on our way out there?" I was hoping that if I said it excitedly enough, she'd agree and come.

When my gaze met hers, I could see her internal struggle. She wanted to say yes, but at the same time, she feared what that meant.

Not wanting her to feel pressured or forced, I shrugged. "Just one friend hanging out with another," I said softly.

Her lips pursed for a moment, and just as I was beginning to settle into the fact that a day at the fair was all she was willing to give and she wanted nothing to do with me, she sighed and nodded. "I guess it wouldn't hurt."

I pumped a fist and cheered. I wasn't going to be shy about how I felt anymore. If I wanted things to progress past Dr. Disaster with her, I needed to start showing her my moves.

It was a fifteen-minute drive to El Azteca for food and another twenty-minute drive from there to the cabin. By the time we got inside and the food dished out, I was starving. We took our plates out to the bonfire pit, and I got busy stacking the wood while Ellise ate.

I had fun lifting the pieces of wood. I made sure to flex while I lifted the logs, just in case she was watching me. By the time the fire was roaring, her plate was half gone and I was just digging into mine. The warmth from the flames washed over me, and the light it cast on her face made my stomach lighten.

I couldn't imagine this night getting any better. Ellise was exactly what I'd been wanting in my life: someone who was smart, strong, and beautiful and blushed when she looked at me. Deep down, I wanted a woman who would care about me because I was Carter, not a

McKnight. And right now, sitting next to her, eating spicy enchiladas, I felt at peace.

"That was delicious," Ellise said as she set her plate down on the ground next to her chair. She held her palms out to the fire and smiled softly.

I murmured in agreement as I shoveled the last bits of rice into my mouth and then reached down to stack her plate with mine. But I didn't move to take the dishes inside. I didn't want her to use that as an excuse to leave. There was a magic that happened around a fire pit. With the night all around and the circle of light holding us close to it —and therefore close to one another—it was like we were in our own world.

The fire had slowed to a low burn, and the sun had set. The sky was dark, but the stars shone against the black tapestry. Ellise tipped her head back, resting it on the Adirondack chair behind her and took in a deep breath. "It's beautiful here."

My gaze was trained on her profile and the way the shadows settled in the crevices of her neck and ears. So much beauty in one person, and my entire body ached to pull her close.

Needing an excuse to touch her, I cleared my throat and stood. "Alexa, play my slow jams."

As Alexa's monotone voice crackled over the speakers that surrounded us, Ellise lifted her head to stare at me. "Slow jams?" she asked.

I loved the way her words rolled off her tongue. She had this way of saying things that made me smile and cower at the same time. She was a formidable woman yet vulnerable in a way that pulled out my Superman side.

"I'm giving you the full Carter McKnight treatment," I said as Jack Johnson's smooth voice carried around us. "Care for a dance?" I asked as I extended my hand.

Ellise paused as she stared at my palm. "Carter McKnight treatment?"

I nodded. "It's a must experience when coming to Evergreen Hollow."

She hesitated, but I kept my ground. I wiggled my fingers in her direction, and finally, she sighed and stood. "If it's a must," she said, but I didn't wait for her to finish.

Instead, I slipped my arm around her waist and pulled her close. My hand found hers and brought it up to rest on my chest. She was so close that the world around me felt as if it were fading away: the crackling of the fire, the hum of the crickets and toads in the darkness, and the ring of trees that lined our property. All that mattered right now was Ellise and me.

I could feel her muscles loosen as I hummed to the music. I tightened my grip on her, reveling in the feeling of her lower back through the soft cotton of her shirt.

"Thanks," I muttered. I didn't know what else to say. I figured proclaiming my intentions to pursue her fully might be too much.

"For what?" she whispered as she peeked up at me.

I held her gaze once I had it. I wanted her to feel the heat of my words. "For coming with me today. It really has been one of the best dates I've had in a while."

Her lips parted and her eyes widened. She wanted to fight me on the word *date*, but I wasn't going to let her. This was a date, even if she wanted to categorize it differently.

"You went with two women," she said softly as she lowered her gaze from mine. I could feel her pulling back, but I held fast.

"I told you, best date ever," I responded with teasing in my voice.

She glanced back up at me and moved the hand that was resting on my shoulder over to swat me. "Hey now."

I shrugged. "Does that bother you that I went with two women?"

She paused as she studied me.

"Because it would be okay if it did." I allowed my voice to lower. I wanted her to feel the weight of my meaning as I held her gaze.

"It would be?" she asked. Her voice was breathy, and it made me smile. I had an effect on her. Which meant she cared.

I nodded. "I can date only you if you want."

Her eyebrows shot up, but I didn't stop. Instead, I brought my hand up from her waist and pushed her hair behind her ear. Then I let my hand linger on her cheek as I stared down at her. I was so mesmerized by the depths in her eyes that we both stopped moving. It was as if we needed as much energy as we could gather to handle the heat flooding our gazes.

"If I want?" she whispered. I couldn't help but study her lips as she spoke. I wanted to touch them. I wanted to kiss them. I wanted her to feel everything I was feeling.

"Yes," I growled, and when her gaze slipped to my lips, I took that as my opening. She wasn't pulling away, so I was going to act.

I pressed my lips to hers for a moment, testing the waters. No matter how soft or warm they were, I forced myself to pull back. She wasn't the kind of girl you just kissed without abandon. I wanted her to know that I was going to wait if she wanted me to.

Her eyes were closed, and her lips slightly puckered. I studied her expression, hoping I hadn't just ruined anything.

Then she sighed. It was soft and sweet, and it caused a racehorse of desire to sprint through my veins.

But I needed to know that she was okay with this. I needed her to say those words. Protecting her had been my goal since meeting her, and I wasn't going to stop now.

"Ellise," I said, my voice throaty and deep.

Her eyes fluttered open.

"Can I kiss you?" I asked.

Her lips tipped up into a smile. "I think you already did."

If this woman only knew. I shook my head. "Not like that. Like, I want to."

Her eyebrows rose, but then her gaze slipped down to my mouth once more. "The Carter McKnight experience?" The teasing in her gaze and smile had me stifling a groan.

"Yes."

She pushed her lips to the side as she raised her gaze heavenward. I was dying inside, and she was teasing me. Then she laughed and nodded. "That's what I'm here for."

With those five words, I threw caution to the wind and pulled her to me. I pressed my lips to hers, channeling all of my desire and feelings into this kiss. She gasped, but when I deepened the kiss, her hands found their way to my neck and tangled themselves into my hair.

I parted my lips, and she did the same. The sensation of her mouth against mine burned like fire inside of me. I scooped her up into my arms and carried her over to the picnic table on the far end of the fire pit.

I set her down and pulled her close to me. I needed the stability the table gave.

I wasn't sure how long we kissed, but I was disappointed when she pulled back. I could have kissed her forever.

"I should probably go," she whispered.

I growled and pressed my hands on either side of her. "Uh-uh."

She giggled as she slipped her hands from my neck, to my shoulders, and down to my chest. I growled and pressed my lips to hers once more.

"I should stay?" she asked.

I nodded. "You should stay."

She wrapped her arms around my neck and tugged me in for another kiss. "Ten minutes. I can stay for ten minutes."

I wanted to complain but decided against it. If all I had was ten minutes, I wasn't going to waste that time. I had much better things planned for her and me. And none of it involved talking.

CHAPTER TEN
ELLISE

"Someone's happy today."

I set the tray of breakfast sandwiches on the counter and reached for a fruit cup. Betty's observation on any other day would have rubbed at my nerves, but not today. "I'm always happy," I replied, even though I knew it wasn't true. I hadn't felt this light, this fun, and this pretty in a long time.

And I had Carter to thank for it.

My ten extra minutes in his arms had turned into thirty because I hadn't been able to bring myself to pull away from his kisses. There was something about him and the way he held me—like I wasn't just a woman who had awakened his desires for a hot piece of meat on a Friday night.

Although I had that feeling too.

The dominant emotions I got from him were honest and real. For whatever reason, Dr. Daydream was into me. And in the quiet parts of my mind, I allowed myself to admit that I was into him too.

Despite all my efforts not to let him into my life, he'd taken up a big space of my thoughts today. I was in the middle of reliving our campfire kissing session when Becky noted the goofy smile on my face.

She gave me an I-don't-believe-you lift of her eyebrow.

I laughed. "Okay, I'm not always happy. But I'm in a good mood today."

She cupped my cheek, bringing to mind my grandmother and the way she used to look at me like I was adorable. "You deserve it." She nodded once. "That sparkle in your eye tells me there's some romance happening, and I want a full report—right after you deliver these breakfast trays. Okay?"

"Okay." I pushed the cart toward the swinging doors and pulled up the delivery instructions up on the attached device pad. My old hospital hadn't had this much tech for the cafeteria. They'd had to do everything with paper printouts, which slowed food service down. I hit the delivery button on the screen, and the room numbers popped up.

I gulped. Of course it would be the maternity ward. Fear, anger, resentment. All of those emotions came rushing back to me, and I took in a deep breath. Why wasn't Betty taking this up? It was her route.

I looked back in time to see her limp to the kitchen door and push through. She'd complained about a hip issue a couple weeks ago. Maybe it was worse and she didn't want to walk the route today.

I groaned. My life couldn't be all moonlight and kisses. My ever after didn't include a *happily* in front of it. No matter how at peace Carter made me feel. No matter how much I wanted to move on from the pain I felt every time I saw the words "labor and delivery," that was never going to happen. And I was a fool to try to make that a reality when there was work to do.

I looked for the bright side—something I used to do out of habit but now had to work at. The chances of running into Carter were much higher if I was in the hallway or the elevator. That would make me smile for sure. I kept my eyes peeled for his broad shoulders in an effort to distract myself from where I was headed. Maybe if I saw Carter, I would feel the strength that came from being near him.

The elevator doors opened, and I let out a deep breath as I loaded the cart. The scent of cooked eggs, toast, and bacon filled the small space. It mixed with the heavy smell of disinfectant making my nose wrinkle. My nerves heightened with each changing number. Any minute now, I was going to go right back to the place I'd been trying to forget.

I hadn't noticed that I was gripping the handle to the dolly until the doors slid open, startling me into letting go. My hands ached, so I shook them out as I peered out onto the floor and I took a deep breath.

The nurses' station was right ahead, and a woman in pink scrubs had her head bent over the computer. I swallowed, sweat forming on my brow. I didn't know what she was charting, but I knew the process. I knew that she'd probably just left a patient's room and checked on the mother and baby. That she'd listened to the baby's heartbeat, counting out the rhythm to make sure the precious bundle was thriving. She'd checked his or her circulation and reaction to light.

There was a part of me that longed to be back with the little ones. The desire peeked every so often through the clouds of anguish that surrounded my soul. Newborn babies were so special, and I swore they came to earth trailing heaven's dust. Despite all the risks, watching them wiggle and coo made all the pain for both mothers and nurses worth it.

I stood there, lost in my thoughts so long that the doors started to close. Worried that I would go down only to have to come right back up and relive this moment over and over, I shoved the cart in the way and there was a loud clanging noise. Cringing, because sleeping babies and tired mommies did not need a wakeup call, I pushed the rest of the way out.

In my desperation to keep the floor quiet, I'd done it. I set foot in L&D. My heart pounded a mile a minute.

"Morning," said the nurse at the station.

"Good morning," I replied as I dropped my gaze. So far, I hadn't had a heart attack, my heart rate was manageable, and my shaking hands were only noticeable by me. To everyone else, I was there to deliver food. And I could play that part. I could do this. I put the image of Carter in my mind, the way he looked at me like I was the most amazing woman on the planet, and pressed on.

"Excuse me?" called a woman from inside an open doorway.

I paused and glanced though to see her lying in the bed on her left side. Her belly was big under the covers, but she looked peaceful. "Is that the breakfast I ordered?"

I glanced at her room number and then to the electronic display that told me which meals went to which rooms. "I'm sorry. But I don't see your room listed here." I used my thumb to scroll up and down.

"I'm so hungry." She rolled onto her back and pushed herself up to sitting. "Can you come in here? I feel like I'm yelling."

I danced from foot to foot, unsure. Being in the hallway was one thing. Being in the room was a whole other level of exposure therapy. It was taking all my strength not to sprint to the elevator, but something caught my eye. This woman looked scared and lonely. Didn't she have anyone who could be with her? Suddenly, the only thing I could think about was helping her feel more at ease.

I stepped just inside the door and put on my old nurse's smile. Funny how it just appeared—like time hadn't gone by at all.

I caught a glimpse of the epidural line snaking up the side of the bed and disappearing behind her. "I'm sorry, but you're not supposed to eat while you're in labor."

Her brow furrowed. "But the nurse helped me put the order in."

I nodded. "They do that so that it's ready for delivery right after you deliver." I grinned, hoping she liked my play on words. Her eyes were growing darker by the minute. Not that she looked ill, but she was ticked.

Too late, I realized she was one of the high-maintenance patients—a mommy diva. I stepped toward the door.

She pointed at me and said, "No."

I froze, not sure what to do. Swallowing, I turned back around and said, "As soon as the doctor gives his approval, I'll bring you something to eat. I promise."

"This is ridiculous!" She screamed the last word and threw a pillow at the wall.

I balked. In the three years I'd worked in L&D, I'd never had a woman throw something. Some yelled. Some screamed. But no one pitched this level of a fit. I glanced over my shoulder at the door and crept backward. "Someone will be here to help really soon. You should try to rest. It's not good for the baby for you to—"

Smack. A notebook hit me in the stomach, and I doubled over. It happened so fast, I didn't have time to block it.

She then let out an ear-piercing scream. I was trying to get my breath back when a doctor shoved past me. "What's going on?"

The scream cut off, and the woman grabbed his coat. "She's being so mean. I just asked when I could eat, and she started screaming at me and told me to shut up." She cried and wrapped her arms around her belly. "She pulled my pillow out and threw it over there."

I stared at her in shock. So many lies.

"You. Outside." The doctor pointed to the hallway.

I stumbled out with him right behind me.

"What are you doing in her room?" he demanded. I didn't recognize him from the cafeteria or anywhere else. He must be new—or a food snob. Though most doctors couldn't afford to be picky. "She's in labor; she can't have food. You shouldn't even be here."

My head finally caught up to what was going on. The trouble was, it was also sprinting to the last time a doctor had yelled in my face that I'd messed up—even though I hadn't. The trauma of the last year built inside of me. It was like this one event brought back everything else. The fear. The shame. The abandonment by friends and even some family. Feeling alone and lost in an unjust world.

"I know she can't have food." The words barely came out as a whisper. My whole body shook, and I couldn't make my throat relax enough to make bigger sounds.

"Get out. You're not our regular delivery person anyway. Send her back up here and leave." His cold eyes stole my strength. I could barely stand, let alone stand up for myself.

Yet I knew I had to move. Numbly, I went to the elevator. The whole world was a fuzzy cloud. All I could see was the button to push and then the sense that the doors had opened. I stepped inside and managed to stay up until the doors closed behind me.

Then I slid down the wall. My chest was too tight, and I couldn't get air.

Oh my gosh, I was going to pass out.

CHAPTER ELEVEN
CARTER

*E*verything felt lighter today. My spirit. My mood. Even my walk.

I tried to ignore Grant's side glances as we made our way to the locker room after a pre-shift workout. But when his eyebrows rose to the midpoint of his forehead, I knew I was going to have to address his burning questions.

"What?" I asked as my smile widened. I'd given up on seeming couth about all of this and let my excitement for Ellise bubble to the surface. I couldn't hide it if I tried, so why try? The woman was amazing, and I'd kissed her—kissed her with everything inside of me, and she'd met me right there. It. Was. Incredible.

"Nothin'. You've just been smiling like the Cheshire cat for the last hour and a half. Apparently, I went too soft on your bench press. I'll note that for next time." Grant turned and used his back to push the door open. He waited for me to enter the room before he let the door swing shut behind him.

My muscles groaned at his response. Soft? Yeah, that was not how I would categorize what he put me through. "The Cheshire cat?" I stopped in front of my locker.

"What?" he fired back at me defensively. "I have a niece, and yes, we've watched *Alice in Wonderland* together."

I shook my head as I pulled open my locker door. "I'm impressed." I thumped him on the back a few times. "You're evolving, my friend."

He shrugged off my hand as he turned to glare at me. "Evolving, ha. I'm still the same old Grant."

I gave him an exaggerated nod before I laughed. The way he took care of Brooke at the carnival shined a spotlight on a sensitive side he was desperately trying to hide. My guess was that Brooke got to him. He liked her, but he was scared out of his mind, and therefore he was overcompensating by diving back into his old ways. "You may be fighting it, but I see your maturity peeking through." I bobbed and weaved as if I were trying to get a better look at him.

He growled and pulled off his shirt, throwing it into the bottom of his locker, where there were several used and abused tee shirts waiting for laundry day. I was pretty sure the cleaning staff dropped disinfectant through the holes of his locker after hours to keep the smell down.

I hurried into the showers and then back out. The sound of Grant's locker shutting followed mine as I turned back to see him glowering at me.

"I'm not ready to hang up my party card just yet," he said as if we could pick up the conversation right where we'd left off.

It took me a second to realize he was hung up on what I'd joked about earlier. Wow. He was deep in it now. What had Brooke done to him?

"But you are," Grant said as he elbowed me in the side. "Don't deny it."

I exhaled as I bent my body in halfway to protect my ribs. Then I glanced up to see him smiling down at me. "Cheap shot," I said as I straightened and pushed my hands through my hair. "But you're right. I'm ready to hand over my party card."

I'd been ready to settle down for a while now. All I needed was the right woman to do it with. And from our kisses last night, I was fairly certain that Ellise was the person I wanted to start down that path with.

"For the cafeteria chick?" he asked.

I nodded, grabbing my white coat off the bench behind me and slipping it on. "Ellise, and yes. For Ellise."

Grant let out a low whistle. "You're in for a challenge," he said. His volume was quieter than normal, which caused me to wonder if he'd intended for me to hear the biting tone to his remark.

He was in the process of slipping his arms through his coat sleeves, and I was trying to figure out why my blood pressure had gone up. Once he'd adjusted the collar, I faced him head-on. "And what does that mean?"

He furrowed his brow for a moment and then nodded his head in recognition. "Nothing, really. It's just … from talking with Brooke, Ellise is a tough nut to crack." He adjusted his name tag hanging on the lanyard around his neck. "I guess she's just not as easygoing as one would think."

First off, Brooke wouldn't say anything bad about Ellise. Which meant that Grant had taken what Brooke did say and sifted it through his party card sieve to come up with that assumption. Second, the cavalier way in which Grant spoke of Ellise, as if she were just another nurse or woman in a group of many, made me angry. Heat began to prick at the back of my neck, and all I could think about was defending Ellise.

A hundred counter points arose—all of them based on the things she'd shared with me. If Grant knew her—really knew her—he'd know she was funny and sweet, and that she truly cared about people. But the broken way she looked when she'd spoken of her past and the way she folded in on herself when she was confronted with that pain had me biting my tongue. Her story wasn't mine to tell.

Grant seemed to sense my frustration and raised his hands in surrender. He shot me a small smile. "I'm not trying to diss of the girl you like; I just want you to be prepared. You may be ready to jump into a relationship with her, but that doesn't mean that she's willing to do the same."

I narrowed my eyes. I didn't like what he was saying—partly because it was true, but mostly because it created a harsh reality compared to the buzz I still had from the night before. When Ellise had opened up to me. When she'd been vulnerable. When all of her worries from the past and why she was here didn't seem to matter.

All that she cared about was me, just like all I cared about was her.

"You don't know her, man," I growled as I moved past him and over to the door. I was ready to get on with my day and completely forget this entire conversation.

"I didn't mean to make you mad," Grant called after me, but I didn't turn around to acknowledge him. Instead, I threw a wave in his direction as the door shut behind me.

Now alone in the hallway, I took a deep breath and leaned against the wall. I closed my eyes and tipped my head back. The familiar smell of cleaning chemicals filled my nose, and I allowed my muscles to relax.

Grant was trying to be a good friend, the kind who was honest even when I didn't want to hear it. In reality, I couldn't fault him for looking out for me, because I would have done the same for him. But I didn't like how it had suddenly become Grant versus Ellise. Why weren't we all on the same side? I liked Ellise. More than I wanted to admit aloud. She was quiet and reserved, but she was also fun and quirky. I just needed to help that side of her come out a bit more.

I needed to help her let go of her past and face the future.

Actually, what I needed was to see her.

No longer content to wait around in the hallway, I pushed off the wall and took the back stairwell down to the cafeteria. I had fifteen minutes before my shift started, so if I wanted to see her, I needed to do it now.

The cafeteria was in full swing. I bumped into a few nurses and a doctor who had trays full of food and had to apologize a few times. They gave me dirty looks, but I brushed them off as I weaved through the hungry crowd, looking for familiar dark hair and dark eyes.

When I came up empty-handed, I located Betty standing behind the soup counter, dishing up minestrone and cream of broccoli. I shouted over the line waiting for a bowl and some crusty bread, "Where's Ellise?"

Betty glanced up to me with the ladle of soup suspended in the air. She threw her head in the direction of the elevator. "Labor and delivery. She went to drop off the lunches."

My stomach soured at her words. Labor and delivery? Today? Ellise wasn't ready for that on her own. Well, maybe she was, but I didn't want her to face all those issues on her own. She should have called me. But she wouldn't, because she was stubborn and strong and capable and independent.

Dang it all—why couldn't she need me just a little bit? It would do my ego so much good.

I sprinted from the cafeteria and over to the elevator. Waiting for it was like watching paint dry. The numbers crept down until the elevator dinged and the doors slid open.

I was ready to run full bore into the elevator but came up short at the sight of Ellise's puffy eyes and sniffling nose. Her gaze was down, so she didn't see me, and for a moment, I wondered what she would do if she discovered that I was standing in front of her.

Would she be embarrassed? Would she pull away?

Could I risk that? Or would it hurt too much?

Feeling like a selfish idiot, I reached out and grabbed her hand.

"Hey—" My words were cut short by her wide-eyed shock. A moment later, she relaxed and allowed me to guide her away from the elevator and into the side supply closet. I tried to ignore the fact that this had been the exact closet I'd caught Jaxon and Lottie kissing in, but for a moment, that memory floated back to me.

Once the door was shut, I flipped on the light and turned to see Ellise sniffling and wiping her nose with a tissue she'd taken from the open box on the shelf next to her. She dabbed at her eyes and then took in a deep breath.

I waited, the silence deafening me. I wanted to know what was wrong. I wanted to know what had happened. And call me crazy, or call it a hazard of the trade, but I wanted to fix whatever had broken her.

I wanted to be the antidote to her pain.

Ellise folded the tissue over and then glanced up to give me a conciliatory smile, sending my heart plummeting. She'd put up a shield and didn't seem to want to let me in. Instead, she emotionally pulled in on herself and offered me a nod of gratitude—as if she was grateful I'd whisked her away so she could compose herself, but she had no intention of filling me in on what had taken her down in the first place.

Every part of me wanted to reach out and never let her go.

"Everything okay?" I asked, breaking the silence. She needed to talk to me. Holding it all in wasn't healthy. I was here. I wasn't going to go anywhere. I could help her face these issues head-on. We could conquer this together.

She sniffled and nodded as she offered me a small, consolatory smile. As if I wasn't going to notice that it wasn't the same as the wide, genuine one she'd given me last night. "I'm fine. Just a little misunderstanding, but I'm all better now."

I blinked as I stared at her. Was she serious? Did she think I would believe her? I knew her more than she gave me credit for. She was hurting, and I wasn't going to let her crawl back into herself and live there, alone.

So I acted. I reached out, wrapped my hand around her wrist, and gently pulled until she crashed into my chest. I took confidence in the way her body relaxed into me and wrapped my arms around her as tightly as I could without crushing her.

"You can tell me," I whispered, my tone low and gravelly. Everything about this woman had my body responding. I wanted to hold her long enough to squeeze out this pain she was holding on to. I wanted to crush any person who wanted to hurt her.

I wanted to protect her like I'd never wanted to protect another human before.

"I'm fine," she choked out before she shook her head and buried her face into my chest.

I reached up and cradled her head in my hand. If she would let me, I would be the man that she deserved.

I wasn't sure how long I held her—I could hold her forever, but eventually, she swallowed and pulled away. She swiped at her eyes and then pressed her fingertips into the palm of her other hand. Desperate to know what she was thinking, I waited for her to look at me before I offered her a smile. "Feel better?"

She pinched her lips together and nodded. "Yeah."

Wanting to lighten the mood and her spirits, I lifted my arms up and pretended to flex. "Yeah, these babies have healing powers."

She glanced between my arms, and just for effect, I made sure to flex them … without making it look like I was trying to. And then she laughed. Loud and deep. Like it came a place inside of her that needed a release.

Minus the fact that she was laughing at my muscles, I reveled in the sound. It wasn't polite, and it wasn't inhibited. This was true and one hundred percent Ellise.

And I loved it.

Her laugh trickled down to a giggle, and a few seconds later, she took in a deep breath and those subsided. Her gaze made its way up to mine, and she studied me. "Thanks. I needed that."

If only she knew how much I needed that as well. "I'm glad I could help," I said with an exaggerated bow.

Her lips tipped up into a smile.

She seemed at ease, so I decided to pry. "Wanna talk about it?" I hurried to add, "My muscles have magical healing powers, but I also have two of these—" I pointed to my ears. "—and they are phenomenal at listening."

She studied me, and then the wall that she'd built up inside of her began to break. Her expression softened, and she shrugged as she slipped her hands into the pockets of her scrubs. "A patient got upset with me and told the doctor that I'd been the one to destroy property when it was her."

"You told him, right?" Rage built inside of me as I stepped closer. Someone mistreated her? Here? In my hospital?

Ellise raised her hand. "I did, but it's fine. I should have known better than to go into a patient's room. I have my place, and I overstepped."

I stared down at her. I couldn't believe her words. From her reaction, I knew that it was more than an offhanded comment. Whatever was said had been cruel and unnecessary.

I had a pretty good idea of who had taken her to task. There was one doctor in L&D that was so full of himself, he'd alienated half the nursing staff. I'd heard complaints about him since the day I'd started. He was within a couple years of his malpractice insurance tripling because of his age—they did that to L&D doctors as they got older, no matter their history. Which meant he'd retire soon. He had years of experience and clout with the higher-ups. He thought he was invincible. But it didn't matter who you were or what job you held. Everyone had a right to courtesy. And what Ellise experienced was not okay.

Her eyes pleaded with me to let it go. I leaned forward and pulled her into another hug. She wrapped her arms around my waist and pulled herself in closer.

I held her a bit longer, trying to show her that I wasn't upset with her. She hadn't done anything wrong. But inside, I fumed. As soon as I dropped her off at the cafeteria, I was on my way up to L&D to let this doctor know exactly what I thought of his behavior.

For the first time in a long time, I was grateful to be a McKnight. Especially here, where the last name held weight and put me on an even level with the doctor who had been here twice as long.

And for Ellise, I was prepared to throw that weight around.

CHAPTER TWELVE
CARTER

The elevator ding might as well have been the bell sounding to start a boxing match, my muscles were so tight. I was itching for a fight, to right the wrong that had been done to Ellise—my girl.

I jerked my head to acknowledge the security guard on duty. He sat next to the desk where he checked in visitors. He didn't seem to pay me any mind as he dropped his bored look back to his phone. I was grateful for this badge at this moment. With it, I was invincible.

My arms were stiff at my side as I charged deeper into L&D. This was a floor of soft sounds and peaceful nap times. It was the place where other doctors came to look for hope in the world when everything went to crap in the ER or operating room. The tranquility poked at me. This should have been a safe space for Ellise to walk into—not a nightmare.

"Where's Mick?" I barked at the nurse standing behind the counter. And then I forced myself to calm down. She wasn't the reason Ellise was in pain. This ridiculous doctor was.

The nurse's eyes widened, and then recognition passed over her expression as she pointed down the hall. Then she half-smiled, like she knew I was going to let him have it and she was grateful that someone was going to stand up to him. "Three doors down on the right. He just went to check on the patient, but he should be done shortly. Then he's all yours."

"Thanks," I threw over my shoulder in her direction as I trudged on. My anger swirled through my thoughts and caused a tornado of words to build up. I wasn't one hundred percent sure what I was going to say, but I knew the gist of what I was going to get across. No one hurt the woman I cared about. Not when she was struggling like she was.

I stood in the doorway of the patient's room and peered inside. Dr. Jerk was standing next to the computer affixed to the wall. He must be looking at a chart, so I cleared my throat and folded my arms as I narrowed my gaze in his direction. "Dr. Mickelson." My tone was firm and only slightly controlled. It wouldn't take much to set me off. But I wasn't going to let this happen in front of a patient. The young woman in the bed deserved to have a peaceful delivery.

Dr. Mickelson flicked his gaze from the screen and then back to me. He sighed as he moved the mouse around. He didn't look interested in speaking to me, and that just angered me more. "Dr. McKnight. What can I do for you?"

Man, had he always had this annoying voice?

"I'd like a word." I stepped back into the hallway without waiting for his answer. The longer it took him to wrap things up and come out, the more frustrated I became with his attitude. I tried to keep calm as I listened as he told the patient she still had a couple hours to go and to get some rest.

He swaggered out, and I reached past him to shut the door. The floor was quiet, and we were relatively alone.

I didn't wait for him to ask me what I needed. I was here to land a blow, and I was going to do that before anything else. "Dr. Mickelson, it has come to my attention that you mistreated one of the cafeteria workers this morning. I'm issuing a formal warning."

His nostrils flared as I watched his confusion morph into recognition. "That woman had no right to talk to my patient."

I stepped up, toe to toe with him. "You had no right to talk to her the way you did." I poked him in the shoulder, itching for the chance to throw a punch. I was heading out of control, and I suddenly empathized with my brother, Mason, when I'd pulled him off a guy at the bowling alley a while back. I hadn't understood how a man could become so angry over a simple comment, but I got it now. "She is a kind, decent person who was trying to help, and you accused her of something she didn't do. Get your facts right, and don't ever talk to anyone on staff like that again."

"Or what?"

"Or I'll have you fired." I spit the words, meaning them with everything inside of me.

"You can try."

I grabbed the front of his white coat and fisted it in my hands, drawing his face so close I could see his pulse beat in the vein on his forehead. His eyes hardened, and his jaw set. "Don't you ever go near Ellise again."

He eyed me coolly as he placed his hand over mine and pushed, trying to get me to release him.

I gripped tighter. "You are nothing more than an overinflated ego. Don't think for one minute that your reputation is beyond my reach. I will see the end of your career if I have to." I shoved him away, and he stumbled before catching himself.

He straightened his white coat and then his tie. "Not if I see the end of yours first." He stormed down the hall. "Jennifer—call Dr. Leon and tell him I'm coming up to see him."

Dr. Leon. The head of the hospital ethics board.

I cursed. Breaking into a jog, I stepped into the elevator with Dr. Mickelson.

He glared at me as he pressed the button for the top floor. "Where do you think you're going?"

I folded my arms. "I have a report to file." He wasn't going to bully me into backing down.

He cringed and quickly rearranged his features.

The best way to stop a bully was to stand up to them. He was going to do his best to make my life miserable, but I didn't even care. So long as he didn't go near Ellise again, it would all be worth it.

I only hoped I had a job when this was over.

CHAPTER THIRTEEN
ELLISE

"Gah!" I threw my purse on the floor by the front door, struggled out of my jacket, and then threw it on top of the purse with a frustrated grunt.

"Bee in your bonnet?" Brooke asked from the couch, where she was working her way through a bag of air-popped popcorn. After the stomachache she'd earned chowing down on fair food, she'd sworn off grease for a week. So far, she'd stuck to the plan, and I was proud of her for it.

"Carter! Ugh!" I threw myself down on the other end of the couch, worn out from being angry all day.

"What did he do?" Brooke turned so she faced me more fully, and I realized she'd dressed up in a pretty wrap dress and long boots.

I furrowed my brow as I was obvious in the way I raked my gaze up and down her outfit. "Do you have a date tonight?" I asked.

She flushed. "No. My boss is throwing a party at his house. I guess it's an annual thing. Everybody's been talking about it for weeks. I have to leave in a half hour, so get talking about Carter—what happened?"

I went limp noodle. "He got in a fight with another doctor because the guy wasn't nice to me, and on top of that, my car is making a noise."

"He got in a fight?" She pushed up so she was leaning over me. Dropping the popcorn bag, she grabbed my shoulders. "He punched a guy in the cafeteria?"

I stared up at her. Trust Brooke not to think about the car. She walked to work each morning. "No! He yelled at him and shoved him in labor and delivery." I wrinkled my brow as I thought back to the many conversations I'd overhead in the cafeteria—not to mention the few people who'd heard my name mentioned and asked me about it specifically. "I spent the whole day telling people I had no idea what was going on or where he was or what had actually happened. One nurse accused me of siccing him on Dr. Mickelson." I threw my hands over my face. "It was horrible. I can still feel them all watching me and whispering." I shivered as if the sounds had brushed across my bare arms.

Brooke sank to her seat. "Wait. Wait. Wait. What happened with Dr. Mickelson?"

I sat up, reached for the popcorn, and began eating as I filled her in on the over-angry, hungry patient and the doctor who catered to her fit.

"Wow. But you made it out without a flashback?"

I paused. A couple weeks ago, I hadn't been able to take trays to the floor without ending up in a ball in the elevator. And today, I'd faced an irrational patient and a doc without falling to pieces. Sure, I'd cried, but I stayed in the present. That was huge for me. "I did." I broke into a smile, the first one I'd had that day. "I did it." My hands shook as I pressed them over my mouth.

I was a long way from working with expectant mommies, but this was a big step for me.

Brooke hugged me. "I'm so proud of you."

"I don't think I could have done it without Carter." The words left my lips before I could stop them. They hung around me as I blinked a few times. It was as if my brain had to catch up with my mouth. My heart picked up speed, and I realized that I might have just let the cat out of the bag.

"I thought you said you went up alone?"

I took a deep breath. Here came the confession that I hadn't wanted to have. "I did. But it was because of him that I felt brave enough to try." I was surprised at how good it felt to tell the truth. Being honest with myself and being honest with Brooke felt ... freeing.

She patted my arm. "Maybe you should tell him that."

I shook my head. I couldn't do that. I couldn't say those things. Then he would know he meant something to me, and I was putting myself at risk. No. I needed to stick to my guns and my frustration with him. "I'm still mad that he went off on the doctor. If he'd kept his mouth shut, I wouldn't be the subject of a thousand rumors or have to testify at an ethics meeting over Dr. Mickelson's behavior."

"Yeah, but I think it's sweet that he stuck up for you. It's about time someone over there did."

I sat with her words for a few minutes. "I don't want him to pity me. I don't want to be his project." The whole idea felt wrong.

"So what do you want from him?"

"I want respect." I wrapped my arms around myself. "I want to be seen as an equal, not the weakling in the relationship."

"Ooh, so we're calling it a relationship now, huh?" She pumped her eyebrows.

I laughed. "Stop it! We're in a ... place." I wasn't quite sure how to explain the fact that the man made my insides swoop with a look, and yet I was so mad at him for today that I could just spit.

Brooke shook her head as she pushed to her feet. "Come on. You need a night out."

"I do? Cuz I thought I needed a night in a bubble bath."

Brooke snorted. "So you can wallow and fume? I don't think so. Go put on that electric blue dress and come with me to my party."

I dragged myself off the couch like a fifteen-year-old who had been asked to empty the dishwasher. "I don't wanna go."

She poked my back to prod me along toward my room. "I hear the food is going to be great."

I perked up. I hadn't eaten anything all day, and to have something I didn't have to cook would be amazing—even if I had to wear a dress and heals. "Okay. I'm going. I'm going."

I turned toward the bathroom so I could wash off the cafeteria smell and make myself presentable. Brooke's boss owned a commercial excavation company and was a great guy. I racked my brain for more information about him, but there wasn't much to find. He was married, I knew that because his wife had given Brooke a blanket for the baby. Oh well, it didn't matter what or who he was; as long as he fed me tonight, I would be his new best friend.

It didn't take me long to shower and slather on some makeup. I grabbed my phone from my work purse. I had a missed call from Carter and three new texts. I stood there, staring at his name. We needed to talk, really talk about a few things, but it would take time. Not knowing what to say to him with Brooke listening in, I tucked the phone in my purse. I'd deal with this tomorrow. "Let's party," I said.

She nodded. "I think you're going to have a great time tonight."

I doubted it. But I smiled anyway. I'd have to face that conversation with Carter soon, because I couldn't put it off and because I wanted to see him. He had helped me be strong, and as much as I hated that I'd needed his help at all, I was grateful he'd been there for me.

Now, I just had to figure out what to do about it.

CHAPTER FOURTEEN
CARTER

"Mom, you outdid yourself." I side-hugged my mom hello as I took in the decorations. My dad threw a pre-holiday party for his employees every year instead of throwing a Christmas party. He figured everyone was busy with family in December and didn't want to sit and listen to him give a state-of-the-company address, so he did it all early.

That was Dad. Always the planner. It was part of what made him a successful businessman, and I admired him for it.

"Thanks. I think it turned out lovely." She hugged me back and then shooed me away. "I have things to do. Don't forget to say hi to your sister—she and Jaxon got in late last night—and your brothers are around here somewhere." Her attention went to a server who carried a large bowl of something out to the patio. "I need to check that." She darted off.

I grinned. If Dad was the planner, then Mom was the heart of our family. I'd come to a party in the house I'd grown up in, and she was trying to make sure I felt at home and had someone to talk to.

I spied my little brother, Liam, first. "Little" was a relative term. The guy was built. As a star on the NFL team the Wolves, he had to stay in shape, but he'd taken it to a whole new level in preseason training and bulked up beyond anywhere he'd been before. He was easy to spot, hanging out near the big screen with a beautiful woman on his arm—one I'd never seen before. I headed that way. The Wolves had a real shot at making it to the playoffs this year.

"Bro!" Liam held out a hand, grabbing mine and pulling me in for a bear hug.

I laughed as his latest girlfriend watched us adoringly.

"Shanice, this is my smart brother—the doctor."

Shanice was even more beautiful up close. She wore a tight dress that showed off her long legs, and her hair was in braids that cascaded down her back. She giggled and held out a hand. "Charmed. Liam brags about you all the time."

I thought about my behavior today and wondered if Liam would brag about that. I was happy that I'd stood up for Ellise and myself after Dr. Mickelson tried to have me fired, but acting like a caveman with an attitude was not my style. I was still trying to figure out what had come over me. "That's because he always wanted to be just like me."

Liam guffawed. He dropped his arm around Shanice and dragged her against his side. "I like my life just fine the way it is."

Shanice blushed. I sort of felt bad for her. Liam wasn't one to hang on to a girl for long. Who knew? Maybe she would be the one to break his streak of girlfriends. I wasn't counting on it, though. My brother was pretty in love with himself. It would take a special woman to beat down his ego.

"You keep telling yourself that, bro." I smiled, told Shanice it was nice to meet her, and then headed out to the patio, where the food tables were. My stomach growled. I hadn't eaten anything all day. My visit with Dr. Leon had taken longer than I had anticipated. He was disappointed in my behavior, and we'd settled it with a warning. Mickelson had some complaints against him, so I had that going in my favor. But I hated the disappointed look in Dr. Leon's eyes, and I'd known right then I needed to be better. I was going to be the best employee, bar none.

By the time I'd gotten out of our meeting, I'd had to run to start my shift and skip lunch to make up for being so late. Staying out of the cafeteria was probably a good idea, since I didn't want to feed the rumors floating around that I was in love with a girl who worked there. I knew Ellise wouldn't appreciate that—even if it was true.

I checked my phone to see if Ellise had returned my texts. She hadn't. I silently cursed. As Superman as I felt for taking on her monster today, I worried that I'd overstepped with her. I didn't think she'd take too kindly to me jumping in uninvited. The trust between us was precarious, and I didn't want to break it.

Halfway through the night, the party was still going strong. I stopped to chat with several of the men I'd worked with throughout the years. It was like walking down memory lane, talking to them. The nice thing about Dad owning a company was that I'd always had a summer job. And construction paid better than fast food. I was feeling good and relaxed as I smiled and laughed.

"Carter!"

I turned at the sound of Brooke's voice and found her sitting next to Grant. His arm was over the back of her chair, and she was leaning into his side as if they were cozy. Too cozy for my liking—especially after the conversation Grant and I had had that morning about turning in his party card. What the heck?

I cocked my head and headed their direction. "I didn't realize you were on the guest list." I squeezed Grant's hand hard.

He gave me a *what gives?* look. "I came looking for you but found Brooke." He grinned.

Yeah, he'd come looking for me, because I'd avoided him all day.

"I told him you'd get around here eventually." Brooke winked at Grant, and he looked at her with something more than interest.

"Can I talk to you for a minute?" I motioned for Grant to follow me over to the buffet. "You cannot play her. She's Ellise's best friend, and she's been through too much crap in her life to have to deal with your party card when she's about to have a baby."

"Whoa." Grant backed up a step as if I'd swung at him. "Watch it. Look, I understand you're upset about what happened with Dr. Mick, but you don't have to take it out on me."

"I'm not upset." I looked down at my clenched fists. "Okay, I may be mad about that. But it's under control. What's *not* is your holding Brooke like you intend for something to happen between you two."

His attention was drawn over my shoulder, and he broke into a wicked grin. "I don't think you should be so worried about me and Brooke—especially when Ellise shows up wearing a dress like that."

I furrowed my brow as I watched his gaze remain fixed on someone behind me. Then slowly, I began to piece his meaning together. Of course Ellise was here. She wouldn't let Brooke go anywhere without her. I wanted to spin around to see if she was actually here, but I didn't. Instead, I turned slowly, and as soon as I saw her, my jaw dropped. Ellise was standing on the edge of the pool, wearing an electric-blue dress that did everything right for her figure. Her hair was down in soft waves, and her makeup was light—just a touch to accentuate her natural beauty. My mouth went dry, and I stopped breathing.

The woman had me wrapped up and tied with a bow.

"You aren't the only one who noticed that dress," Grant said besides me.

My attention shifted to the males around the pool, and I found my hound-dog expression mirrored in their looks. Oh, heck no!

I took off for Ellise without looking back at Grant, who hooted with laughter. I couldn't go another minute without being near her, and we had a whole lot to talk about. I just hoped my brain functioned properly, because with her in that dress, I was not thinking about putting words together.

CHAPTER FIFTEEN
ELLISE

I felt like an idiot, standing by the pool and trying to look as if I belonged. Everyone around me was laughing or whispering, and I was pretty sure it had nothing to do with me, but my mind kept going to that place.

Did they know I didn't belong at a party like this? I was a tailgate-and-hot-dogs kind of girl, and this house and party were all about showing off the zeros in a checking account. I mean, I'd had no idea that Brooke worked for such a wealthy family. The house. The food. The pool. I was pretty sure they didn't eat ramen noodles on the floor in their living room while watching TV on a cracked screen.

That had been my childhood. Not pool parties or play dates.

"You look beautiful," a low, smooth voice said behind me.

My hackles rose, and I turned, summoning the fire in my belly. I was going to confront this creeper. I had no intentions of being hit on today. None whatsoever.

"Listen, buddy—" I started, but as soon as I met the laughing gaze and cocked smile only Carter could give me, the anxiety left my body in a whoosh. My brain stopped working, and as a result, the only thing I could do to save face was pinch my lips closed and drop my gaze. There was no way I wanted him to see what his presence did to me.

"Buddy?" he asked, obviously not letting go of what I'd just said. "Is that my new nickname?"

I forced a chuckle as I turned away from him. I kept my focus on the ripples in the water. Two adorable kids swam at the shallow end, and they seemed less intrusive to watch than turning to face the man who had my insides tied up tighter than rope. He was just silent and completely at ease. How did he do that?

"Why are you here?" I asked. Out of all the houses and all the parties, why did he have to show up here?

Carter furrowed his brow as he studied me. "McKnight Construction?" He waved his hand toward the house. "I grew up here."

I parted my lips as they formed an O. Of course. The difference between us highlighted what I'd been mulling over that day in my anger and then even after the anger subsided—I needed to finish this journey on my own. I was too broken to be good for Carter. One episode in L&D and he'd put his job on the line. That wasn't fair to him, and I couldn't drag him deeper into my trauma and expect him to come out unscathed.

He looked sheepish as he gave me an awkward smile. "I'm sorry." His words came out a whisper, and I wondered for a moment if I'd heard correctly.

"What?" I asked, turning to face him out of habit. In nursing school, they always emphasize how important it was to keep your body facing your patient. That way, you could read things about them that they might not be able to verbally convey.

But the movement caused me to come inches from his chest. Apparently, when I'd turned away, he'd moved closer. I'd misjudged his distance, and that left me closer than I wanted to be. Especially since feeling his warmth and smelling his cologne reminded me of how close we'd been. It reminded me of the feel of his lips on mine. Of his arms wrapped around my waist, holding me close as if he never wanted to let me go.

And in that moment, I didn't want him to let me go either.

It took a breath for the shock to wear off so I could remember how to move my body again. I stepped back and wrapped my arms around my chest. I needed the added protection that the embrace gave me. It protected my heart from him. It provided the barrier that I needed.

"I'm sorry," he said again. His gaze was cautious as he shrugged. His hair fell down over his forehead, and it took all of my strength not to reach up and brush it away.

Another reason it was a good thing that my arms were tucked safely across my body: I could ward off these ridiculous desires to touch Carter. If I was honest with myself, they were stronger than I cared to admit.

I needed to focus. "What do you have to be sorry about?"

He furrowed his brow as he studied me. "Did you not..." He raked his hand through his hair. I had to admit, he looked good when he was nervous. "I mean, I thought you heard what people were saying."

I kind of wanted to play dumb just for a while longer. I liked seeing him rattled. It made him more human to me. But then I felt bad for teasing him, so I just smiled and nodded. "No, I heard. Something about the cafeteria worker finally taming the rogue doctor." I raised my eyebrows as I met his gaze.

"Tame the rogue doctor?" His cheeks flushed as he glanced around. "People are crazy."

I nodded. "You're right. They are." I sighed. I was ready to focus on what we really needed to talk about. I was ready to face this and move on. Sure, I liked Carter, but I wasn't ready for him. I didn't want him to be my knight in shining armor. I wasn't even sure who I was anymore, and I needed time to figure it out.

I sighed and moved toward the pool house. I figured some privacy was in order. "Come on," I called over my shoulder.

I made my way to the far side of the house. There, the music was faint and no one lingered to hear our conversation. By the time I was tucked up next to the corner, Carter was only a foot behind me. I stopped and turned. He stopped as well and glanced around, confused.

"What?" he asked slowly as he raised his eyebrows.

I shot him a look. "I thought we could have some privacy while we talked."

He let out a nervous chuckle as he nodded. "Yeah. I knew that. I didn't think you were trying to kill me or anything."

"Naw, I'd take you camping and kill you." Then I leaned closer to him and dropped my voice. "No witnesses, and it's easier to claim that you fell." When I pulled back, I saw that his eyes had widened considerably.

"Wow. You've thought a lot about that."

"I like watching *Unsolved Mysteries*."

He chuckled. "Strangely, so do I."

Our laughter died down, and soon, we were right back where we were before: confronting what had happened earlier in the day and also facing what our future held. I hated having to always come back to my past, but the truth was, I was too broken right now to be with anyone. I just didn't know how to tell him that.

"I let things go when it came to Mickelson." Carter shoved his hands into the front pockets of his jeans as he shrugged. "I should have been better. I am better. I just …" He paused as he studied me. "I just don't like people hurting those I care about."

My entire body warmed at his confession. I wanted to brush it off and pretend I didn't hear it. But that wasn't true. I knew what he said, and so did he. But he didn't seem as hesitant as I felt. He looked certain. Like saying the words he'd just said was as easy as breathing.

Why wasn't he scared like I was?

I needed to pull back and regroup. "Listen, I appreciate what you did for me. You've helped me a lot. I feel more confident about facing my issues, and for the first time, I actually had hope that I would be able to walk back onto the L&D floor with confidence." I took in a deep breath.

"Is this supposed to be a bad thing?" he asked, interjecting before I could say more. His smile was soft, but I could see a spark of fear behind his gaze. And I hated that. I hated that I was hurting him.

But it was better for him to walk away now than get in too deep and hurt even more.

"I'm not in a place where I can do ... this," I said, my voice breaking with emotion.

He took a step closer to me, and all I could do was extend my hand to keep him at bay. When his abs met my palm, he stopped. He dropped his gaze to where we collided, and then, slowly, he dragged his eyes up to meet mine. "You don't mean that."

The emotion and depth in his voice made my entire body want to reject the words I'd just said. I wanted to throw caution to the wind and embrace him. I wanted to fall in love with Carter, I did. But I was too scared. Scared that I was so broken, I would never be able to be the person he thought I was. Or the person he needed me to be.

"I do," I whispered as tears began to form. "I really do mean them." As those words left my lips, a tear escaped and rolled down my cheek.

Carter knitted his eyebrows together, and I could see him chewing on my words. He looked as if he were fighting with himself on whether he should step toward me or walk away.

I wanted to break down and take the turmoil away, but I didn't want to give him false hope. I'd already made that mistake, and I cared too much about him to do it again.

It took a moment before he sighed and nodded. He smiled, but only to mask the pain. I knew I should walk away, and I was going to. As soon as we got back to the party, I was going to call a cab for Brooke and me, and we were going to leave for good. I wished I'd brought my car, funny noise or not.

Carter held up a hand. "Let's just enjoy the party for tonight. Tomorrow, if you never want to see me again, then I'll go away. But we both need some downtime."

"Carter, I—"

"As friends." He gave me a hopeful smile. "I promise. Just as friends."

I studied him. Why was he doing this? Why was he being so nice to me? He should hate me. Throw me out of this house like the imposter I was. His life had been simple before me. Why did he want to prolong our suffering?

Because I was suffering. I hated the idea of not seeing him each day, of never being in his arms again. It ate at me like battery acid, but there was nothing I could do about it. I'd have to live with aching for him so he could have a better life.

Realizing that I owed it to him to stick around for a while after all he'd done for me, I nodded. It was the least I could do. Literally, the very least. Because I could take back everything I'd said and rip the Band-Aid off for both of us, but he wasn't ready for that. He needed some time to ease out of … us. I could give him that. If he wanted me to linger, I'd stay. Just for tonight.

"Okay," I said softly. "As friends."

He offered me a weak smile as he nodded and turned. I followed after him and back into the party. People were playing pin the heart on the Grinch—after a few drinks, it got very interesting to watch. The laughter filled the silence around us, and even though I wanted to relax, I knew I couldn't. I was going to spend the rest of the party holding my breath and waiting for that last goodbye.

We made our way through the crowds. Carter introduced me to some of his friends, and we engaged in small chat. It was awkward, but Carter seemed determined to keep me here and involved in conversation, so I slapped on a smile and did my best to look entertained by golf stories and the latest trends in construction materials. I wasn't sure why, though. It would be easier for him to enjoy himself if he wasn't trying to get his friends to talk to me.

"Mom," Carter said to a woman with graying hair and a blinking ugly Christmas sweater on. She held a tray of pigs in a blanket and laughing at what a taller, more muscular version of Carter was saying. "Dad, I want you to meet Ellise."

My entire body froze as Carter's mother's gaze swept over me. Her smile widened as she shoved the tray toward the Carter look-alike next to her and reached out and pulled me into a hug. I didn't have time to react; instead, I found myself crushed against her. She smelled of lilacs and bacon, and her hug was so tight that it pinned my arms to my side. There was something magical in a mother's hug. They were full of acceptance and happiness that you were on the planet. I wanted to sink into it and let it scrub away all the feelings of not being wanted I'd gathered at my old job. I thought I'd dealt with them before, but they were still there—maybe not as bad as they had been. Time helped. Carter had helped. Now his mom was doing her best, even if she didn't know it.

How I wished I could be part of this family.

"Welcome, Ellise," she said when she pulled back. There was a twinkle in her eye that caused me to miss my own mother—but only for a moment. My mother was nothing like Carter's mom. And missing her was not something I was going to start doing.

"Thanks," I said, not sure how to respond to her overwhelming welcome. She stared at me like a woman who had found her salvation. I glanced at Carter. Did his mom want him married off? If so, he hadn't said anything. Not that my-mom-says-I-have-to-get-married was an easy conversation to have with a woman who was trying to keep you at arm's length.

"Ellise is Brooke's friend ... and my friend," Carter said. "This is my mom and dad, Brenda and Joseph McKnight."

His mom nodded as she ran her gaze over me. "We love Brooke here in the McKnight house. Did she get the blanket I sent over? I wished she'd tell us the gender, 'cause then I could finally pick up some of the outfits I've been tempted over." She sighed. Just like a grandmother would. Which made me like her more. She was the kind of woman who was the mother to everyone and the grandmother to every baby.

"I personally think it's going to be a girl. Brooke leans toward that clothing section whenever we pass by." I grinned.

"I hope so. I adore ruffles."

"Me too." My smile came easier. The more time I spent with Brenda, the more I liked her. Dang it.

"Have you talked to Penny?" Carter asked. "You could always buy Katie something."

I furrowed my brow, and Mrs. McKnight must have noticed, because she leaned into me. "Katie, the little one in pigtails in the pool, is Penny's." Then she turned her attention back to Carter. "She's sleeping. Poor girl is just so tired lately. I think it's the moving back and forth between California and here."

"But nothing about news?" Carter asked slowly.

Mrs. McKnight shook her head. "No. No news. Why? Do they have news?"

My eyes went wide. Penny was pregnant. I just knew it. The sallow look to her skin when she'd come to check on Brooke. Being extra tired and sleeping through a party. It all added up. I also realized that Brenda didn't have a clue.

Carter's skin paled, and he was quick to shake his head. "Nope. News? Not that I've heard." Then he glanced around for a moment before his hand wrapped around mine and I was being pulled away from them. "What did you say, Lottie? I'm coming," he called to a beautiful blond woman standing with a mountain of muscles. I blinked. Was that Jaxon Jagger? Holy cow—the NFL star was one of my and Brooke's favorite impossible crushes. I mentally cringed. I'd have to take him off the list tonight. No way I could meet his girlfriend—fiancée?—and not feel guilty checking him out.

Carter half dragged me across the patio and over to a couple who were standing by one of the tiki torches, laughing. "This is my baby sister. She's dating my other brother's best friend."

"Are they engaged?" I half hated that I had to ask. I didn't want to know. Although if anyone would make a good husband, it was Jaxon. He was a Boy Scout.

"Yes. Wedding's this December."

Lottie glanced from me over to Carter. "I didn't call you over here."

"I know, but I needed to get away from Mom before she ... pries more."

A knowing look passed over Lottie's face as she took in me and our clasped hands. "Yeah. Mom can sniff out a secret better than a hound dog. I'm Lottie, Carter's sister. We'll keep whatever secret you have safe. Right, Jaxon?" She elbowed the hulk of a man next to her.

He harrumphed and nodded. "My lips are sealed."

Feeling the need to correct their assumption, I raised my hand to speak, but Carter beat me to it. "Ellise and I are just friends."

It was weird. It sounded wrong as he said it. But I knew that was unfair to even entertain that thought, so I gave Lottie a small smile.

She didn't look convinced, but thankfully, she didn't push it further. Instead, she nodded and then turned her attention to Carter. Someone shouted Jaxon's name, and they excused themselves to go greet them.

I sighed as I glanced over at Carter. I knew what he was trying to do. He was trying to hold on. I should know. After all, hanging on to the thing that hurt me was something that I was used to. And it was killing me inside.

If I cared about him like I did, then *I* needed to be the person that pulled the bandage off. It was the only way we were going to heal like we needed to. If I didn't leave now, I feared that I was never going to.

"I should go," I said as I started walking backward.

Carter's eyes widened, and I could see him moving to follow.

"No. Please, just let me go." I raised my hand to emphasize my words. He needed to stay put.

"Ellise—"

"Goodbye, Carter." Tears clung to my lids as I turned and hurried to where I'd seen Brooke sit earlier. There was no way I could hear what he had to say and survive. My heart was shattering into a million pieces.

I found Brooke despite the haze from the tears. As soon as she saw me, she stood, said goodbye to Grant, and wrapped her arm around me. I felt like an idiot being escorted out of the party by my pregnant friend, but right now, I needed her support. I was floundering here.

We climbed into a cab that had just dropped someone off. Brooke snuggled in next to me, holding me as I let the tears flow. She didn't ask me what was wrong or what had happened. Instead, she held me and let me cry.

This was why we were best friends, and right now, I needed my best friend.

I was walking away from the guy that I was pretty sure I'd grown to love.

I was breaking.

Maybe that was why I didn't notice her tense. We were only a few blocks away from the McKnight mansion when she let out a cry. I lurched up and saw the puddle growing. "Pull over!" I yelled at the driver.

CHAPTER SIXTEEN
CARTER

And just like that, she was gone.

I stood next to the refreshment table, staring at the spot where she'd once been. I felt like an idiot as everyone tried to move around me, but I didn't care. She was gone, and my heart was broken. These partygoers were just going to have to deal with me being the traffic stop.

"What happened?" Grant asked as he stepped up next to me. He was holding two drinks in his hands and was sporting a very confused expression.

I sighed as it turned toward the table and pulled a croissant from the pile in front of me. I ripped off a corner and shoved it into my mouth. I chewed with aggression. It felt good to work my frustration off on something, even if that something was just a French baked good.

"One minute we were fine, and the next she was gone. All I did was go talk to the bartender for a minute." He shrugged.

I stared at him. What was he talking about? "She broke up with me and left," I said, feeling a tad confused as to why he was so interested in where Ellise had gone.

Grant mirrored my expression; he looked exactly how I felt. "Brooke broke up with you?"

"No." Realizing we weren't getting anywhere, I raised my hand. "You're talking about Brooke?"

He nodded.

"Oh. I'm talking about Ellise. She stormed out on me, taking Brooke with her."

Grant looked disappointed. "Well, that's a bummer." He set down what looked like some fruity ice drink onto the table. "I had the bartender mix this special."

"You got a margarita for a pregnant woman?" I knew he hadn't gotten all As in med school, but he had passed.

"Har har. It's a virgin one." He glanced around the party with literally dozens of single, beautiful women. "Now who am I going to talk to?" He sighed.

Wow. He really liked Brooke. I'd never seen him pine for a woman. "Me?" I answered. I could really use a friend right now.

Grant's gaze scanned me before he sighed. "I'm screwed." I punched his arm, and he moved to protect it. "Ouch." He gave me a dirty look. "Do you think abusing me is going to get you what you want?"

My entire body felt heavy as I realized that there was no way I was even remotely getting what I wanted right now. I was alone, and I was always going to be alone. I'd found Ellise, the perfect girl for me, and she'd walked away.

"Aw, man, I'm sorry. I didn't mean to make you upset." He glanced behind me and waved.

I turned to see that Grant had summoned Mason and Sadie over. They were holding hands and smiling bigger than I cared for. I mean, I was happy they were together. I knew they'd gone through a lot to get to where they were today, but seeing them so over the moon for each other was like salt in my wound.

It stung.

"Hey," Mason said as he extended his hand, and we did the shake-to-hug thing that Mason was known for. He was just finishing up the program he'd gone through to help him deal with his PTSD, and he was trying to be more physically affectionate because of it.

"Hey," I said when we pulled back. Liam's old friend Heather had been instrumental in getting him into treatment. I was grateful she'd been willing to step in, and I had recommended her to one of my patients since.

I nodded at Sadie, who slipped her hand back into Mason's. "How's things with Ellise?" She turned to look at Mason as if she were asking if she got the name right.

I stared at both of them. "How do you know about Ellise?" Had the rumor mill made its way out of the hospital?

Mason nodded over to Mom, who was talking to Heather.

I groaned. That wasn't good. "Mom told you?" I growled. "I told her Ellise was just a friend."

I zeroed in on Mom and headed in her direction just as Mason called out to me, "You know Mom—there's no such thing as 'just friends' with her."

I threw an acknowledging nod in Mason's direction as I stepped up to Mom.

"Perfect, here he is now," Mom said as she wrapped her arm around my waist and pulled me in next to her.

"Mom, what are you telling people?" I asked low, not wanting to bring a lot of attention m way—especially since Ellise had stormed out.

Mom laughed. "What are you talking about?"

"Mason asked me about Ellise. Said you told him?"

"See?" Mom waved toward me as she moved to include Heather in the conversation. I hated that she was talking like I wasn't even here.

"I do," Heather said as she nodded. "Classic denial."

I balked. "What now?"

"It's strange, right?" Mom went on as if I hadn't spoken. "He's so convinced that she's not his girlfriend, and yet, I can see how much she means to him." Mom sighed. "I'd love your advice for both of my single boys. Are they afraid of commitment?"

Heather tipped her head as she considered me. "I don't think Carter has a commitment issue, but Liam …"

A storm raged inside of me. I loved my mother, I did, but this wasn't the time for her matchmaking shenanigans. "We're just friends," I repeated, but I knew it was going to fall on deaf ears.

Mom nodded and patted my chest as she moved away, taking Heather with her. Apparently, she was ready for Heather to assess Liam. Which I was fine with, but I was not okay with both of them leaving while still under the impression that Ellise and I were anything but what I said we were. Friends.

And I wasn't even sure we were that anymore.

My phone rang, and I pulled it from my back pocket. I didn't even wait to see who it was from. I just brought it to my ear. "We're friends," I exclaimed again. At least with whoever was on the other line, I would have their undivided attention.

There was a sniffle, and suddenly, the world around me faded.

Ellise.

"Carter?" she asked, her voice sounding small and fragile.

"What's wrong?" My overprotective drive was on full acceleration. I felt as if I could run to wherever she was like Superman.

"It's Brooke. She's in trouble."

I didn't wait for her to say more. Instead, I grabbed my keys from my pocket and raced to the parking lot. On my way out, I called to Grant that he should get to the hospital and get ready. He looked confused but nodded. It must have been the crazed look in my eye that convinced him not to ask questions. Having him on duty in the ER would give me peace of mind. Not that he should work on Brooke; his emotions were too involved where she was concerned. But I needed backup.

By the time I was in my car and on the road, I was in full panic mode. Not only for Brooke, but Ellise. She sounded so small, and it was taking all of my self-control not to speed. I'd already pushed my luck for her when I'd gone after Mick; I couldn't count on my police officer brother to fix a ticket for me too.

The good news was, she wasn't that far away. She'd only been gone ten minutes. My foot pressed down on the pedal, and my car responded smoothly. Ellise was breathing, and I could hear Brooke panting in the background. I drove as if I was headed to their place, hoping I was on the right route.

When I finally saw the taillights of the cab on the side of the road, I let out my breath. It was only a matter of seconds before I could get in there and take over. I pulled in behind the cab, threw the car into park, and grabbed my case of supplies from the back seat. I didn't even bother to turn off the engine. I jogged over.

Brooke moaned as Ellise crouched down on the ground outside the car by her legs. "You're okay, Brooke. You're okay," she chanted, her eyes wide and not focused on anything in front of her.

The driver looked white as a sheet. His arm was folded across his chest, and his hand was brought up to his lips. He looked completely out of his element.

"What happened?" I asked. I opened the bottle of sanitizer and began to slather my hands with it.

The man parted his lips but didn't say anything.

Realizing that he wasn't going to be any help, I moved to stand behind Ellise and placed my hands on her back. "I'm here," I said.

Ellise froze and then glanced up at me. Relief filled her face. I could tell she'd been crying, and for a moment, I wondered if it had been because of me or because of Brooke. And then I felt like a jerk. Of course it was because of Brooke.

"Her water broke," Ellise said quietly as she moved out of my way.

"Was it clear?" I asked.

When Ellise didn't answer, I turned to see that her eyes were wide, and she shook her head.

I swore under my breath. That wasn't good. But it was workable. The baby was definitely coming, and we weren't going to be able to wait. "Brooke, it's Carter. I'm going to check to see how far you are dilated. Your baby might have inhaled some of the meconium. We need to get it out as soon as possible." I slipped on a pair of gloves and threw my stethoscope around my neck.

Brooke's body tensed, and she moaned in response. I waited for the contraction to pass before I checked her.

"Nine centimeters," I whispered. Things were moving too fast for a first-time mom. She may have been in labor for a while but thought they were more Braxton-Hicks. Dang it.

"I called 911. Where are they?" The cab driver swore under his breath as he paced behind me. He had a cleaning bill coming up that wasn't going to be pretty.

"We don't have time. The baby is coming." I jerked my head for him to move to the back of the car. "Stand over there and watch for them, though. I need you to flag them down."

He took the job, grateful to be away from the stress happening in his back seat.

Brooke let out a wail, and her entire body began to shake. She was entering into active labor, and the baby was coming.

"Ellise," I said as I stood and rested my hands on her shoulders, turning her to face me. She looked panicked and refused to meet my eyes. "I need you to help me." I shifted so that she couldn't avoid me.

"I can't. I can't," she repeated under her breath.

I pulled her to my chest and held her there. Regardless of what this meant for us, I wanted her to know that I was here. That I knew she was stronger than she thought. "You can," I said. "Brooke needs you. I need you. You can do this."

For a split second, I felt her face rest against my chest, and I allowed my eyes to close. I knew why she'd walked away. I knew why she was scared. And I wanted her to know that she never had to be afraid with me.

She pulled back a moment later and nodded. "I'm ready," she whispered.

The wail from Brooke didn't leave me room to respond. Instead, I headed back to my patient, who was panting through her contraction. The delivery was fast. In a matter of minutes, I was crouched down on the ground with a tiny, slippery baby girl in my arms.

Ellise was up in the driver's seat, holding Brooke's hand. They were crying as Ellise told Brooke how she'd done a beautiful job and that she had a baby girl—just like they'd hoped. Brooke looked exhausted but grateful that the pain was over.

With nothing to wrap the baby in, I quickly unbuttoned my shirt and slipped it off. Her lungs were clear, and she wailed louder than her mama had bringing her into this world. I laughed at the sound, so relieved that she was going to be okay.

I tried my best to wipe the baby down before I handed her over to the waiting arms of Ellise so I could help Brooke with the placenta.

Ellise smiled through the tears as she held the little one close to her chest to listen to her heart and her lungs. She was doing what she'd been taught to do, and I'd never seen her more at peace.

The sound of sirens and the blue and red lights filled the darkness and broke the spell that the little one had cast over all of us.

As soon as the paramedics jumped out, I was pushed to the side. They got Brooke onto a gurney. She was smiling but tired as she held the baby in her arms. I gave the paramedic a quick summary as they hoisted Brooke into the ambulance. They recognized me from the ER and commented on how lucky Brooke was that I'd happened to come along.

I shook my head in response. This wasn't about being a hero—it was about helping a friend.

Ellise lingered by my arm, and I could tell she wanted to say something. But I didn't want her to brag me up or try to break up with me again. Either way, they weren't the words I wanted to hear. Not right now. Not when there was so much hope in the world at the sound of that baby's cry.

I wanted her to go with Brooke so that this moment wasn't spoiled. Whenever I looked back on it, I'd see Ellise's radiant face as she took the baby from me and cooed. It was a piece of heaven.

"Carter, I—"

"It's fine. Go. Brooke needs you." I stepped back, not ready to confront the woman who'd just broken my heart a half an hour ago.

Ellise hesitated but then nodded. "Thanks."

I waved away her response and then trailed after her as she made her way to the ambulance and climbed in next to Brooke. Just before they shut the door, I made eye contact with Brooke. "Grant's waiting for you at the hospital. I'm sure he's in full panic mode. I didn't tell him what was going on."

Brooke nodded but wasn't able to respond as the paramedic shut the door on her.

I waited as they drove off. Once they rounded the corner and were out of sight, I sighed and glanced over at the cab driver, who looked like some of his color was coming back. I reached out to clap him on the shoulder, but then I saw the gloves on my hands and decided against it. I slipped them inside out as I pulled them off.

"I'll be going," I said as I saluted him.

If the cab driver heard me, he didn't move to respond. Instead, he muttered under his breath as he climbed into the driver's seat and drove off.

Now officially alone, I made my way back over to my idling car and climbed in. I didn't drive home. Instead, I went back to my parents' house. Even though I looked as if I were walking out of a horror movie, I didn't care. There was no way I wanted to be alone tonight.

Mom's mouth fell open when I walked into the house. She hurried over to me, but I just waved her off.

"Everything's fine. I'm taking a shower and then going to bed." I didn't bother to meet her gaze. There was no way I wanted her to see how broken I was because I'd lost Ellise. Seeing her in action tonight only made me love her more and made being without her that much worse. I wasn't ready for the mom conversation. I knew it was going to end with her telling me that I was a great guy, and if Ellise couldn't see it, then she didn't deserve me.

"Okay," Mom whispered.

I was grateful that she wasn't going to push me further.

After I showered and climbed into bed, I shot a quick text to Grant asking how Brooke was. He sent me a smiling emoji followed by a picture of him holding the baby up like Rafiki in *The Lion King*. He looked happy, and I felt jealous.

He and Brooke seemed like they were heading somewhere, and

that idea made me happy. But inside, deep inside where I didn't want to acknowledge it, I felt angry.

Angry that it should be me.

Sad that it would never happen.

Not when Ellise was determined that we were over.

My happiness was gone, and I doubted it would ever come back.

Just call me Dr. Perpetually Single, because that was who I was destined to be.

Forever.

CHAPTER SEVENTEEN
ELLISE

"She is the most perfect being on the planet." I buried my face in the baby's tuft of soft black hair and breathed in her brand-new person scent. Despite her rather dramatic entrance into the world, Pumpkin—as I was calling her until Brooke picked a name—had slept the night away and hardly made a peep.

Of course, it wasn't like her mother or I let go of her for any longer than to allow the nurses to do their jobs, so she'd had it pretty cush since being born.

Grant had stayed late last night. He just couldn't get enough of holding Pumpkin and alternated between staring at her in awe and staring at Brooke. What a strange place they were in to start a relationship, but if it worked for them, then I was all for it. Grant had a reputation, but I couldn't picture the guy who changed Pumpkin's first diaper being the player who dated a different woman every week. Time would tell.

What surprised me most was how calm I'd been this whole time. I knew that being here should freak me out, and at times it did, but nothing like it had when I first got here. I was finding a feeling of peace about my past that I had doubted was even possible. There was something about Carter that had calmed my pain and helped me realize there was a light at the end of the tunnel. My tunnel. My tunnel of fear.

"Knock knock," came a soft call from the open doorway. I looked up from my charge to see Brenda McKnight holding a bright pink bag with tissue paper popping out the top. "Can I come in?"

My blood froze. I'd broken up with her son last night—I was the last person she wanted to see, and yet here she was. What was the proper protocol for this situation? Leaving. That would be best. I could excuse myself, and all the awkwardness would go with me.

I went to stand so I could hand Pumpkin to Brooke, but Mrs. McKnight waved for me to relax as she came over and bent down to inspect the baby. "Well, isn't she stunning?"

Brooke beamed. "I think so."

"Me too," I added. I'd hardly had a minute to think about the delivery and Carter swooping in to save the day. I'd frozen in place, my training a hundred miles away, until Carter had arrived. His calm had fueled my calm and allowed my instincts to take over. It was hard, especially since the effect he had on me only proved that I was totally and completely in love with him and couldn't do a thing about it.

I was split in two minds where I wanted to run to him and hide all at the same time. That was why I was holding Pumpkin so tight. She was the only thing grounding me in reality.

"I heard you had an exciting delivery." Mrs. McKnight sat on the armrest, looking comfortable and still poised. Did women grow into that sort of elegance after surviving children, or were they just born that way?

"Did Carter tell you?" Brooke looked at me too quickly and then away. I hadn't told her what happened between the two of us before we'd left, but I could tell she had questions. After all, I had dragged her away from the party and then cried all over her shoulder in the cab before she'd gone into labor. I knew I was going to have to fess up, but thankfully, Pumpkin's arrival overshadowed the demise of my romance.

"Actually, there's a news story floating around." Brenda smiled. "They interviewed the cab driver. I'm sure the hospital is keeping your identity a secret, though." She reached down and tucked the blanket under Pumpkin's chin. "I brought you both a gift." She handed the bag over to Brooke, who proceeded to pull out a full layette—in pink—and lay it around her on the bed like she was decorating a Christmas tree.

Brooke's eyes filled with tears. "It's too much." She gulped as she swiped at her eyes; the tears didn't show any signs of slowing down. "I can't—" Gasp. "—accept it."

Mrs. McKnight moved over to the bed and put her arms around Brooke. I softly bounced Pumpkin in sympathy for her mom's tears. "Of course you'll accept them." She rubbed Brooke's arm and reached for the tissue box at the same time. The woman had mad mothering skills.

"I'm sorry. I think it's the fear coming out. I was so scared something was going to be wrong with her. And then she came so fast. I didn't—I couldn't—" Brooke blubbered.

"Oh, honey, of course you were scared. Life's best moments come with a dash of fear." She let Brooke cry for a second.

In light of my recent issues, her words had snagged in my mind's net and wouldn't shake loose. "What do you mean?" I pressed, holding the baby tightly to my chest. "What good moments come with fear?"

"Oh, you know." Mrs. McKnight flapped a hand. "People get cold feet at weddings. New babies overwhelm." She turned to look at me. "Even falling in love is like strapping on a parachute."

I dropped my eyes to the baby. "Not if you don't leap," I mumbled as I kissed her soft head.

Brenda fussed over Brooke, smoothing her hair off her face and dabbing at her cheeks with a tissue. "Look at you. You lived through the scariest moment of your life and came out of with a precious baby girl. You're strong. You're a fighter. And I know this girl is going to grow up to be just like you."

"Let's hope she's a little less bossy," I quipped as I got to my feet and offered Pumpkin to Mrs. McKnight.

Brooke laughed and then started crying again. She fanned her hands at her cheeks. "I can't seem to turn it off."

Brenda settled into the chair I'd just left, a peaceful and contented look on her face as she held Pumpkin. She looked like a natural grandmother. For a moment, the idea of her holding *my* baby in her arms entered my mind. But then I pushed that thought out. In order for her to be holding my baby, that would mean Carter would be the father. And that was not a thought that was going to heal my already breaking heart.

"You're totally normal," I told Brooke, moving my attention away from my ridiculous thoughts and focusing on my friend. "I, however, am not." I didn't take my leap. I scurried back from the door and settled into a ball in the corner of Brooke's bed.

"That's normal too," said Carter's mom. "The question is, what do you do about it now?" It was almost as if she knew what I'd done. Had Carter told her? Did she hate me?

I put an arm around Brooke, letting her lean on me while she tried to dry out. I'd done the same for dozens of women who came through L&D. It felt good—right, even—to be a part of my friend's big day. "I don't know. How do you love a person when you're broken?" I'd meant the question to be for me, but when I released it in a whisper, I waited to see if someone would answer.

"Oh, honey." Brenda's tone was full of compassion and an eye roll. "If we waited until we were perfect to love someone, no one would ever get together. I mean—*men*, right?"

We all chuckled at that one.

"They leave their clothes *next to* the hamper, their dishes *next to* the sink, and their cars parked *just outside* the garage. Perfection is not a requirement for love." Her smile was wide and genuine.

Her words settled around me, making me feel less crazy. I chewed on my lip as I thought about what she said. "I'd just like to feel strong for once." I stuck out my lip. "I don't want to be his project."

"Trust me, he'll be yours too. That's what a relationship is." She glanced down and traced Pumpkin's chubby cheek. "You're both working to make yourself and each other happy. It's a huge, lifelong project—but the benefits are worth it."

We stared at Pumpkin, and she broke into a yawn and stretched, her skinny arm popping out of the blanket.

Brenda was right. No one could be perfect, and everyone brought baggage into a relationship. The thing was, my baggage seemed a lot heavier than Carter's. Then again, he'd almost gotten in a fistfight yesterday, so maybe he had issues too. But I'd noticed something at his house last night that I was just starting to put together. No family, no matter how much money they had, was free of pain. The McKnights certainly had their share. Even though there were happy couples just about everywhere I'd looked, they each had a story.

I wanted a chance to write mine—with Carter.

If he'd let me.

Brooke nudged me. "What do you think?"

I smiled. "I think she speaks the truth."

"So what are you going to do about it?" Brooke pushed me, and I slid off the bed and onto my feet. I guessed that was her way of hinting that I needed to go find Carter.

"I'm going to go home and brush my teeth."

"Ellise!" She grabbed for me.

I danced out of the way. "I'm kidding. I'm going to find Carter and ask him to be my boyfriend." I dared a glance at his mom.

Brenda's smile was hard to miss. She didn't look disappointed or shocked. Instead, she pumped her free hand in the air while shouting, "Finally!" Scooting back in her chair, she spoke to Pumpkin. "Maybe I'll be back here in a year with a little friend for you—hmmm?"

Had she read my thoughts? My whole face burned, and Brooke burst out laughing. Which started her tears again. "Shoot!" She reached for the tissue box.

"I'll send the nurse in with more tissues." I waved as I made my way out the door, a smile on my face.

As soon as I was alone in the hallway, I took a deep breath. The fear was back, but now that I knew it was part of all this—part of life's big moments—I realized how amazingly big it was that I'd found someone to love in the middle of the hardest year of my life.

Which meant that Carter was a pretty special guy to see past all that and find my heart.

I clutched my chest, hoping I wasn't too late and that I hadn't ruined everything.

CHAPTER EIGHTEEN
CARTER

The cabin was silent as I stood on the deck and stared out at the lake in front of me. I took in a deep breath and allowed my heart to feel as if it were constricted despite the excess room. My thoughts returned to Ellise and the look of fear in her eyes as she'd stared at me. And the way we'd worked together to help Brooke birth her baby—there was something there, I was sure of it.

Ellise cared for me, just like I cared for her.

Well, cared was too light of a term. I loved her. Wholly and completely.

I wanted to tell her. I wanted to shout it from the rooftops. I wanted to wrap my arms around her and hold her to my chest. I wanted to be the support she needed to move on from her trauma. She was stronger that she knew. She didn't need me to fix her problems; I knew that. She just needed someone behind her to help hold her up.

And I could be that for her. If she'd ever let me.

I'd moped around Mom and Dad's house all morning until Mom had informed me that she was heading to the hospital to see Brooke. One look at my downturned expression, and she'd sat me down and asked me what was wrong. I'd wanted to keep it in, but the words had flowed from me and I hadn't been able to stop until I'd told her everything.

My thoughts, my feelings. The pain I was experiencing. I'd laid all of it out in front of her and hadn't held anything back.

Mom had been quiet. She'd given me a long hug and told me to hold on; she could see the sun breaking soon.

I'd wanted to ask her what she meant, but she hadn't elaborated. Instead, she'd given me a kiss on the head and disappeared out to the garage with a gift in hand and a ridiculously optimistic smile across her lips.

Not wanting to hang around the house alone, I'd grabbed the keys to the cabin and split. Mom seemed to think it would all work out, but I had doubts—whale-sized ones.

I scrubbed my face and took in a deep breath. This was my future. The sound of birds and frogs and nothing else. I was going to be alone, forever.

Not wanting to wallow anymore, I turned and headed back inside. Just as I slid the door to the outside closed, there was a knock on the front door.

I paused and leaned forward to see if, in fact, I'd heard right.

A knock came again.

Well, I'd been right. But who would be here? One of my siblings might have come out to check on me. More likely, Mom had sent Heather out here to rescue me like she'd done to Mason. The last person I wanted was that redhead poking around my psyche.

I pulled the door open. My gaze swept over Ellise, and for a moment, I wondered if I were seeing things.

"Ellise?" I asked, and then I felt stupid. This was obviously a mirage. And I was the lunatic talking to it.

"Hi," she whispered.

I stumbled back. She was actually here. My entire body heated as I took her in. Her cheeks were flushed and her gaze hesitant. Her smile was soft as she glanced around. She held a white plastic back to her side, and she kept fiddling with it.

"Can I come in?" she asked.

I wasn't sure what to do, so I nodded and moved away from the door. "Did you come to kill me?" I joked, thinking of our *Unsolved Mysteries* comments.

She chuckled. "Sorry, wrong-sized bag." She pointed to the sack she carried.

Once she was inside, she stood in the entryway as I shut the door. When she didn't move to come in further, I motioned to the bag. "So no body parts to throw in the lake?"

She glanced down and then back up at me. My joke had fallen flat —or rather, she wasn't in a joking mood. She shook her head. "Actually, I'm here to talk to you."

I folded my arms and leaned against the nearby wall. "Talk to me?" I raised my eyebrows.

She nodded. "Yeah."

A silence fell over us. I waited for her to continue, and when she didn't, I waved my hand toward her. "I'm all ears."

She held the plastic bag between both hands now, and I could see her grasp was tight. She was nervous. Why?

Hating to see her so uncomfortable, I moved to take control. "How's Brooke and the baby?" Besides some mushy texts, I'd been able to get very little out of Grant.

Ellise nodded. "She's good. Adorable and perfect. Brooke is tired but content." Her expression softened like it always did when she was talking about her friend. "She hasn't picked a name, so I dubbed her Pumpkin."

I smiled lightly. I could see Ellise throwing that one out and Brooke agreeing. If the little one wasn't careful, she'd have Pumpkin on her birth certificate. "I'm happy to hear that."

"I want to jump."

Her words tumbled out so fast that I had to pause to make sure I'd heard right. I leaned into her. "You want to jump?"

She pinched her lips together, and her cheeks flushed. Her eyes were wild now as she glanced around. She was fighting something, but I wasn't sure what.

"Where do you want to jump?"

"With you." Then she closed her eyes and shook her head. "I want to jump with you."

"With me?"

She nodded and then opened her eyes again. "I don't want to be alone anymore. I want ... you."

Those three words hit my ears like a Mack Truck. I hesitated, not sure if I'd just blocked out the other words or she'd actually said them together, in that sentence and in that order. "You ... want me?" I motioned toward my chest just so I could clarify who *you* was in this conversation.

She pinched her lips together and nodded. "Yes," she whispered. "I want you."

Emotions clung to my throat, making it scratchy. I cleared it, hoping to dislodge them, but it didn't work. My heart pounded, and all I could see in front of me was the woman I wanted to love forever.

Throwing caution to the wind, I acted. I crossed the space between us and wrapped my arms around her. She laughed as she dropped the plastic bag and hugged me back.

"Are you sure?" I asked as I buried my face into her hair. It smelled amazing.

She nodded into my chest. "I'm sure. I know I'm broken and I have work to do. But I also know that there isn't anyone else that I would rather work on myself with than you."

I pulled back and stared down at her. I didn't drop my gaze as I peered deeply into her soul. "I love you," I said, my voice husky and low. I didn't care. She had to know I meant my every word.

A tear slid down her cheek as she nodded. "I know. And I love you back."

I leaned down and crushed my lips to hers. She responded by wrapping her arms around my neck and rising up onto her toes to deepen it. I lifted her up, feeling like we were jumping as my stomach swooped in pleasure.

Our kiss said everything that we couldn't. The pain, the sorrow, the fear. It all melted away as we fell into feeling of the other person.

When I pulled back, we were both breathing hard. Her lips were swollen and her cheeks were flushed, but this time, I could tell it was from happiness instead of fear.

I set her back down on the ground but kept her pressed against me. I wanted to feel her. I needed to know she was there. "Are you sure?" I asked, peering into her gaze.

She chewed on her bottom lip and nodded. "Ninety-nine point nine percent sure."

I chuckled as I kissed each of her cheeks, her chin, the tip of her nose, and then brushed my lips against hers. "I like those odds."

She rose up to meet my lips, and this time, our kiss was deeper and more passionate than ever before. When I went to swoop her legs with one arm and pulled her up to my chest, she giggled and moved away from me.

"Where are you going?" I growled.

She laughed as she reached down and picked up the bag she'd brought in. "We can't forget these."

I furrowed my brow as I swept my arm at her knees and pulled her up to my chest. "What are those?" I asked. There was nothing more interesting to me at this moment than Ellise.

She opened the bag and nodded toward the inside. "Take a look."

I paused and glanced in. "Candy bars?"

She giggled. "You said it's a must."

I tightened my grip on her as I brought her into the living room. We collapsed on the couch with me under her as she sat on my lap. She turned to run her hands through my hair, tracing her fingers along my cheeks and then to my lips.

I growled as I leaned in closer to her.

"So what do you say?"

I frowned. "About what?"

"Having a redo of our first date?"

I shook my head. "I don't want that."

She looked confused. "You don't?"

"Nope. I want to date you now. I don't want to go back in time. I want to look forward to my future—" I leaned in and kissed her. "—with you."

She sighed as she nodded and leaned her forehead in to rest on mine. "I want that, too."

"Do you trust me?" I asked.

"I do."

"Then that's all that matters."

We kissed again, this time not breaking to speak. Instead, we lost ourselves in the feeling of the other person in our arms and pressed against our bodies.

Ellise was all I wanted, now and in the future. And if she trusted me, then I had the strength to move forward.

We were in this as one.

We were in this together.

She was my person, and I was hers.

Forever.

EPILOGUE

"You told my mom I have commitment issues?"

I glanced up from my computer screen to find Liam McKnight glowering at me. He pressed his fists into my mahogany desk and growled.

I wasn't gonna lie; that was sexy and made my lower belly quiver. But I'd been fighting off these feelings for as long as I'd known Liam, and I wasn't about to let them run over the top of me now—especially in my office.

Working out of Evergreen Hollow Memorial was a boon to my practice. Not just anyone could get this kind of real estate as a fledgling psychiatrist, but my work with Mason McKnight gave me a few strings to pull. And man, had I pulled hard. I was all about making it in this world and earning a name for myself as I helped people work through their traumas. I was going to be someone, darn it. Someone respected in this town instead of part of the no-name family I'd been born into.

"You do have commitment issues." I pushed back from my chair and rounded the desk, the sound of my three-inch heels clicking on the polished wood floor in time to Liam's short breaths.

His eyes raked over my tight, though professional navy wrap dress, which set off my red hair beautifully. I might have been an awkward teen with freckles and uncontrollable curls, but growing up looked good on me. For a moment, I wondered if I'd made it to the level Liam set for his short-term girlfriends. Models. Actresses. Socialites. They all had one thing in common: they looked good on Liam's arm.

I shook myself. I didn't care if I looked good on his arm—I wanted to look good standing alone. But old habits died hard, and I snipped off the bit of jealousy before it could take root.

Liam stood up and folded his huge arms. Seriously, did the man take steroids? He couldn't. The NFL would ban him if he did. So all that was natural. *Hmm.*

"I like dating. There's nothing wrong with that."

"True. But you're a habitual dater. You can't stand to be alone—yet you can't commit to a woman." I tipped my head and ran my eyes over him as he'd done to me just moments before. "If you ever want help with that, let me know. The diagnosis was on the house."

He growled again.

I willed my knees to stay strong as I made my way back to my chair. Lifting my almost unnecessary glasses to my face, I raised an eyebrow. "If that's all, Mr. McKnight, I have a full docket of patients to see today." I started typing nonsense just so I looked busy.

"Stay away from me." He flipped around and slammed my door behind him.

I collapsed in my seat—hating that he still had that effect on me after all these years. I shouldn't want him at all, especially not after seeing the trail of women he left in his wake. I refused to be one of them. I figured I had one thing going for me that those other women didn't—a big IQ.

I, Heather Campbell, would never fall for the charms of Liam McKnight.

I glanced at my screen to see what I'd typed and dropped my head in my hands.

There, in black and white, were the words "Dr. Heather McKnight."

I was in so much trouble.

Return to the McKnight family series where Liam finds out that his commitment issues have more to do with his romance coach than he thought.

Click here to get your copy, today.

ABOUT THE AUTHOR
ANNE-MARIE MEYER

Anne-Marie Meyer lives south of the Twin Cities in MN. She spends her days with her knight in shining armor, four princes, and a baby princess.

When she's not running after her kids, she's dreaming up romantic stories. She loves to take her favorite moments in the books and movies she loves and tries to figure out a way to make them new and fresh.

Join her newsletter at anne-mariemeyer.com

ABOUT THE AUTHOR
LUCY MCCONNELL

Lucy McConnell loves romance. She is the author of the Billionaire Marriage Broker Anthology and contributes to the Snow Valley Anthology and the Echo Ridge Anthology.

Her short fiction has been published in *Women's World Magazine,* and she has written for *Parents' Magazine* and *The Deseret News.*

Besides fiction, Lucy also writes cookbooks. You can find her award-winning recipes under Christina Dymock.

When she's not writing, you can find Lucy volunteering at the elementary school or church, shuttling kids to basketball or rodeos, skiing with her family or curled up with a good book.
You can sign up for her newsletter—and get a **free book**—by going to https://mybookcave.com/d/290d4f96/

You can find more of her romances by clicking here.

authorlucymcconnell.wordpress.com